PPF

CW01655141

Throne of Dragons

BOOKS BY MORGAN RICE

AGE OF THE SORCERERS

REALM OF DRAGONS (Book #1)

THRONE OF DRAGONS (Book #2)

BORN OF DRAGONS (Book #3)

OLIVER BLUE AND THE SCHOOL FOR SEERS

THE MAGIC FACTORY (Book #1)

THE ORB OF KANDRA (Book #2)

THE OBSIDIANS (Book #3)

THE SCEPTOR OF FIRE (Book #4)

THE INVASION CHRONICLES

TRANSMISSION (Book #1)

ARRIVAL (Book #2)

ASCENT (Book #3)

RETURN (Book #4)

THE WAY OF STEEL

ONLY THE WORTHY (Book #1)

ONLY THE VALIANT (Book #2)

ONLY THE DESTINED (Book #3)

ONLY THE BOLD (Book #4)

A THRONE FOR SISTERS

A THRONE FOR SISTERS (Book #1)

A COURT FOR THIEVES (Book #2)

A SONG FOR ORPHANS (Book #3)

A DIRGE FOR PRINCES (Book #4)
A JEWEL FOR ROYALS (BOOK #5)
A KISS FOR QUEENS (BOOK #6)
A CROWN FOR ASSASSINS (Book #7)
A CLASP FOR HEIRS (Book #8)

OF CROWNS AND GLORY
SLAVE, WARRIOR, QUEEN (Book #1)
ROGUE, PRISONER, PRINCESS (Book #2)
KNIGHT, HEIR, PRINCE (Book #3)
REBEL, PAWN, KING (Book #4)
SOLDIER, BROTHER, SORCERER (Book #5)
HERO, TRAITOR, DAUGHTER (Book #6)
RULER, RIVAL, EXILE (Book #7)
VICTOR, VANQUISHED, SON (Book #8)

KINGS AND SORCERERS
RISE OF THE DRAGONS (Book #1)
RISE OF THE VALIANT (Book #2)
THE WEIGHT OF HONOR (Book #3)
A FORGE OF VALOR (Book #4)
A REALM OF SHADOWS (Book #5)
NIGHT OF THE BOLD (Book #6)

THE SORCERER'S RING
A QUEST OF HEROES (Book #1)
A MARCH OF KINGS (Book #2)
A FATE OF DRAGONS (Book #3)
A CRY OF HONOR (Book #4)
A VOW OF GLORY (Book #5)
A CHARGE OF VALOR (Book #6)
A RITE OF SWORDS (Book #7)
A GRANT OF ARMS (Book #8)
A SKY OF SPELLS (Book #9)
A SEA OF SHIELDS (Book #10)

A REIGN OF STEEL (Book #11)
A LAND OF FIRE (Book #12)
A RULE OF QUEENS (Book #13)
AN OATH OF BROTHERS (Book #14)
A DREAM OF MORTALS (Book #15)
A JOUST OF KNIGHTS (Book #16)
THE GIFT OF BATTLE (Book #17)

THE SURVIVAL TRILOGY
ARENA ONE: SLAVERSUNNERS (Book #1)
ARENA TWO (Book #2)
ARENA THREE (Book #3)

VAMPIRE, FALLEN
BEFORE DAWN (Book #1)

THE VAMPIRE JOURNALS
TURNED (Book #1)
LOVED (Book #2)
BETRAYED (Book #3)
DESTINED (Book #4)
DESIRED (Book #5)
BETROTHED (Book #6)
VOWED (Book #7)
FOUND (Book #8)
RESURRECTED (Book #9)
CRAVED (Book #10)
FATED (Book #11)
OBSESSED (Book #12)

Throne of Dragons

(Age of the Sorcerers—Book Two)

Morgan Rice

Copyright © 2020 by Morgan Rice. All rights reserved. Except as permitted under the U.S. Copyright Act of 1976, no part of this publication may be reproduced, distributed or transmitted in any form or by any means, or stored in a database or retrieval system, without the prior permission of the author. This ebook is licensed for your personal enjoyment only. This ebook may not be re-sold or given away to other people. If you would like to share this book with another person, please purchase an additional copy for each recipient. If you're reading this book and did not purchase it, or it was not purchased for your use only, then please return it and purchase your own copy. Thank you for respecting the hard work of this author. This is a work of fiction. Names, characters, businesses, organizations, places, events, and incidents either are the product of the author's imagination or are used fictionally. Any resemblance to actual persons, living or dead, is entirely coincidental. Jacket image Copyright zeferli used under license from istockphoto.com.

Morgan Rice

Morgan Rice is the #1 bestselling and USA Today bestselling author of the epic fantasy series THE SORCERER'S RING, comprising seventeen books; of the #1 bestselling series THE VAMPIRE JOURNALS, comprising twelve books; of the #1 bestselling series THE SURVIVAL TRILOGY, a post-apocalyptic thriller comprising three books; of the epic fantasy series KINGS AND SORCERERS, comprising six books; of the epic fantasy series OF CROWNS AND GLORY, comprising eight books; of the epic fantasy series A THRONE FOR SISTERS, comprising eight books; of the new science fiction series THE INVASION CHRONICLES, comprising four books; of the fantasy series OLIVER BLUE AND THE SCHOOL FOR SEERS, comprising four books; of the fantasy series THE WAY OF STEEL, comprising four books; and of the new fantasy series AGE OF THE SORCERERS, comprising two books (and counting). Morgan's books are available in audio and print editions, and translations are available in over 25 languages.

TURNED (Book #1 in the Vampire Journals), ARENA 1 (Book #1 of the Survival Trilogy), A QUEST OF HEROES (Book #1 in the Sorcerer's Ring), RISE OF THE DRAGONS (Kings and Sorcerers—Book #1), A THRONE FOR SISTERS (Book #1), TRANSMISSION (The Invasion Chronicles—Book #1), and THE MAGIC FACTORY (Oliver Blue and the School for Seers—Book One) are each available as a free download on Amazon!

Morgan loves to hear from you, so please feel free to visit www.morganricebooks.com to join the email list, receive a free book, receive free giveaways, download the free app, get the latest exclusive news, connect on Facebook and Twitter, and stay in touch!

Select Acclaim for Morgan Rice

"If you thought that there was no reason left for living after the end of THE SORCERER'S RING series, you were wrong. In RISE OF THE DRAGONS Morgan Rice has come up with what promises to be another brilliant series, immersing us in a fantasy of trolls and dragons, of valor, honor, courage, magic and faith in your destiny. Morgan has managed again to produce a strong set of characters that make us cheer for them on every page.... Recommended for the permanent library of all readers that love a well-written fantasy."

—*Books and Movie Reviews*
Roberto Mattos

"An action packed fantasy sure to please fans of Morgan Rice's previous novels, along with fans of works such as THE INHERITANCE CYCLE by Christopher Paolini.... Fans of Young Adult Fiction will devour this latest work by Rice and beg for more."

—*The Wanderer, A Literary Journal* (regarding *Rise of the Dragons*)

"A spirited fantasy that weaves elements of mystery and intrigue into its story line. *A Quest of Heroes* is all about the making of courage and about realizing a life purpose that leads to growth, maturity, and excellence.... For those seeking meaty fantasy adventures, the protagonists, devices, and action provide a vigorous set of encounters that focus well on Thor's evolution from a dreamy child to a young adult facing impossible odds for survival....Only the beginning of what promises to be an epic young adult series."

—*Midwest Book Review* (D. Donovan, eBook Reviewer)

"THE SORCERER'S RING has all the ingredients for an instant success: plots, counterplots, mystery, valiant knights, and blossoming relationships replete with broken hearts, deception and betrayal. It will keep you entertained for hours, and will satisfy all ages. Recommended for the permanent library of all fantasy readers."

—*Books and Movie Reviews*, Roberto Mattos

"In this action-packed first book in the epic fantasy Sorcerer's Ring series (which is currently 14 books strong), Rice introduces readers to 14-year-old Thorgrin "Thor" McLeod, whose dream is to join the Silver Legion, the elite knights who serve the king.... Rice's writing is solid and the premise intriguing."

—*Publishers Weekly*

TABLE OF CONTENTS

Chapter One 1
Chapter Two 6
Chapter Three 12
Chapter Four 17
Chapter Five 23
Chapter Six 28
Chapter Seven 33
Chapter Eight 38
Chapter Nine 42
Chapter Ten 47
Chapter Eleven 52
Chapter Twelve 57
Chapter Thirteen 62
Chapter Fourteen 67
Chapter Fifteen 72
Chapter Sixteen 79
Chapter Seventeen 83
Chapter Eighteen 91
Chapter Nineteen 96
Chapter Twenty 101
Chapter Twenty One 106
Chapter Twenty Two 111
Chapter Twenty Three 115
Chapter Twenty Four 121
Chapter Twenty Five 126
Chapter Twenty Six 132

Chapter Twenty Seven 137
Chapter Twenty Eight.....................................142
Chapter Twenty Nine 147
Chapter Thirty 153
Chapter Thirty One 157
Chapter Thirty Two 162
Chapter Thirty Three.....................................167

Chapter One

When Lenore woke, for one beautiful second, she thought that it had all been a nightmare. She could feel the softness beneath her, and she saw the simple comfort of the inn's room, and she assumed that the awful things she remembered must have been no more than the terrors of the dark. They couldn't be real, they...

They were. Lenore knew it a second later as consciousness came back to her, knew it in the bruises and the pain. She shook her head, trying to *make* herself not think about where she was, but she could no more hold back those thoughts than she could hold back an ocean.

The Quiet Men King Ravin had sent for her had kept her here, a prisoner. When she'd tried to break free, they'd beaten her. Eoris and Syrelle were the worst...

Lenore forced herself to look around, to think of anything else but this.

The room at the top of the inn was empty now except for her, and Lenore knew this might be the only chance she would get to survive this. Shaking, having to ignore the pain with every motion she made, Lenore started to stand.

She fell against the bed for a second, catching herself, but she didn't fall back. If she let herself fall back, she wouldn't get up again, and then she would just be waiting for them to carry her away to King Ravin's lands.

I will be strong, she told herself.

She made her way to standing. She didn't look much like a princess now. Her dress had tears in it from the violence of her capture, but Lenore pulled it back on anyway, tying the torn elements together as best she could.

She padded toward the door on silent feet. Outside, she could hear Eoris and Syrelle talking, and Lenore's heart hammered in her chest, fearing that they might be about to come back inside.

"... sure we don't have time to tarry here with the princess?" Syrelle asked, in that wheedling, half mad voice of hers.

"We need to get her back to the south, my love," Eoris said. "And if you hurt her too much she won't transport easily."

"King Ravin is no fun," Syrelle said.

"And when I tell him you said that, what do you think he'll do to you?" Eoris shot back. "No, we leave in an hour. We'll head for the nearest bridge and be across soon enough. Remember to leave some of the maids alive. King Ravin wants them to talk."

He wanted them to talk? Lenore found herself caught between happiness that at least some of her servants were still alive and horror at all the things they must have suffered alongside her, fear of how many of them might have died, and confusion, because why would King Ravin want *any* of them alive to tell people that he had King Godwin's daughter?

That didn't matter right then. The only thing that mattered was trying to get away. She'd tried that before though, and hadn't gotten even as far as the stables. How was she supposed to get away when she'd already been caught once, when they had shown that they could catch her whatever she tried?

No, she wouldn't give up, she couldn't. Once they got her beyond the river... how could anyone hope to escape from there? It *had* to be now, while they were occupied; while they still thought that she was helpless and caught here.

Knowing that there was no way out through the door, Lenore went over to the window. It was chipped and sticking, hard enough to open that Lenore was sure it would creak and protest as she pushed the shutters apart, giving away what she was doing to anyone listening. Lenore opened it and froze in place, waiting to see if there was any reaction. No one burst into the room though, no one shouted or raised an alarm.

Lenore looked over the ground below her. There was a low roof for the floor below, and beyond that the open space beyond the inn, with a courtyard leading over to the stables. There were bodies in that now, dragged into a pile as if they were mere refuse, something that didn't matter at all to the Quiet Men who had killed them. Lenore could see some of those Quiet Men now, no longer dressed in peasant garb, but in dark leathers and dulled scale armor that made them look ready to fight an army's worth of foes.

One, a woman, was standing over a group of four of Lenore's servants. She pointed to two and set them running, far enough away that Lenore couldn't see which ones they were. Then she raised a small, hand-sized crossbow.

"No," Lenore whispered to herself in horror, even as the first bolt flew out. It struck the first servant in the middle of the back and she fell, tumbling into the dirt. She rose up, screaming, looking back toward the one who had shot her...

That only meant that the second bolt took her through the chest.

Lenore wanted to scream too, her heart breaking at the sight of an innocent girl she'd thought of as almost a friend being butchered for no reason. She *didn't* scream though, because then it would have been over; there would have been no way to escape. She focused on the one who was still running, knowing that at least one of them was going to get free.

Lenore waited until she saw that the Quiet Men were all moving in different directions, looking to their preparations to leave rather than at her. When she saw her moment, Lenore screwed up her courage and stepped out of the window. She crunched down onto the roof of the overhanging section, hoping against hope that it would bear her weight.

She moved to the edge of the roof in a crouch, checked that there was no one beneath, and tried not to catch her breath at the sight of the drop below. She could do this; she had to. Swinging off the side of the roof, Lenore hung on by her hands for a moment, took a breath, and dropped.

She hit the ground hard, the breath coming out of her in a whoosh of air that was only good because it stopped Lenore from crying out loud enough to be heard. She rolled to her knees, waited for her head to stop spinning, and forced herself to stand once again. She managed to get up and started into the shadows of the next building.

She didn't try for the stables this time. There were too many Quiet Men around it, and no hope of getting a horse clear of them without being spotted. Instead, Lenore knew her best hope was to make her way away from the inn on foot, staying in the trees and bushes near the road and hoping that one of her brothers would be coming with the forces that should have been there to protect her in the first place…

Why hadn't they come? Why hadn't they been there to save her? Vars had been sent to protect her, and Rodry had said that he would take over the duties partway around the wedding harvest, yet neither of them had been there when Lenore needed them. Now she was alone, having to sneak out of the village and hoping all the time that she could avoid the Quiet Men for long enough.

She kept going; it wasn't far now. Just a few dozen paces, and she would be out of the village. Once she was in the open ground beyond, surely even the Quiet Men couldn't find her?

That thought was enough to make her keep going. Lenore crept from the shadow of one building to the next. She was almost there, almost there.

There was a patch of open ground ahead of her, and Lenore froze on the edge of it, waiting, looking left and right. She couldn't see anybody, but she knew already how little that could mean with people like this. But if she stood there and did nothing…

Lenore ran as much as she could, given how her body hurt with every step, bursting forward for the safety beyond the open ground. Behind her, she heard a shout from the inn, and she knew that Eoris or Syrelle had gone into the room where they'd left her, discovering her missing. The thought of them in pursuit was enough to make her move faster, running for the greenery beside the road, for hiding, for *safety*.

"There!" a voice called, and she knew then that they'd spotted her. She kept going, not knowing what else to do, knowing only that if she stopped, they would have her in their clutches again.

She couldn't run any faster, but she was at least among the trees and the bushes beside the road now, her breath coming in pants as she ran, moving left and right in an effort to foil her pursuers.

Lenore heard the sound of footsteps behind her and dodged around a tree, not daring to look back. Another tree lay ahead, and she knew that if she could only get around it, there was denser greenery beyond. She could lose them there, maybe, but first she had to choose. Left or right... left or right...

Lenore went left, and immediately knew that it was the wrong choice as strong hands grabbed her, weight bearing her down to the ground hard, knocking the breath out of her. She tried to fight, but she already knew how little she could do. Hands wrenched her hands in front of her, tying them there, then pulled her up.

The man who stood there was Ethir, the one who had caught her in the stables; the first one who had... He lifted her easily, setting her on her feet.

"You're going to regret running, Princess," he said in that soft voice of his. "We'll make sure you're going to regret it."

"Please," Lenore begged, but it made no difference. Ethir dragged her back toward the waiting horses, and the trip south, and every moment of horror that awaited her beyond the bridges leading out of the kingdom.

Chapter Two

King Godwin II of the Northern Realm sat on his throne in front of a sea of his courtiers and struggled to keep his temper. After all that had happened, after his daughter Nerra had been forced to leave, he hated that he still had to sit here, pretending that all was well. He wanted to rise up from this throne and go after her, yet he knew he couldn't.

Instead, he had to sit here, in a great hall that even now had the remnants of the feasting before not quite cleared away, holding court. The great hall was huge and stone built, with banners on the wall with the bridges that marked the North. Squares of carpet had been set out, each one restricted to a different rank of the nobility, or to particular noble families.

He had to stand there before them, and he had to do it alone, because Aethe wouldn't step out in front of courtiers who had helped send Nerra away. Right then, Godwin would have preferred to be almost anywhere else: Ravin's kingdom, the third continent of Sarrass, anywhere.

How could he pretend when Nerra was banished, and his youngest daughter, Erin, seemed to have run off to be a knight? Godwin knew he looked disheveled, his graying beard less than perfect, his robes of office stained, but that was because he had barely slept in days. He could see Duke Viris and his cronies looking over with obvious amusement at that. If the man's son weren't due to marry his daughter...

Thoughts of Lenore calmed him. She was off about the wedding harvest, accompanied by Vars. She would be back soon, and all would be well. In the meantime, though, there were serious matters that needed to be attended to; rumors that had swirled through the court and promised danger for all of them.

"Bring forward my son!" Godwin said, the words ringing around the room. "Rodry, step out here and be seen!"

His eldest son stepped out through the crowd of those watching, looking like the knight that he was, and like the man Godwin had been when he was younger. He was tall and muscled with years of sword practice, his blond hair cut short so as not to get in the way. He was every inch the warrior, and it was clear that people watched him with love as he strode through them. Now, if only he could *think*, as well.

"Is all well, Father?" he asked, offering a bow.

"No, all is not well," Godwin shot back. "Did you think I wouldn't find out about the ambassador?"

Say this for his eldest son; at least he had a solid streak of honesty in him. He could no more hide behind a lie than behind a slender tree. Vars would probably have dissembled out of cowardice, and Greave would have wrapped everything up in pretty quotes from those books of his, but Rodry just stood there, solid as a stone. With about the brains of one, too, given what he said next.

"I couldn't just stand there after he'd insulted our entire family, our whole *kingdom*," Rodry said.

"That's *exactly* what you should have done," Godwin shot back. "Instead, you shaved his head, *killed* two of his guards... If you weren't my son and heir, you'd hang for something like that. As it is, those friends of yours..."

"They took no part in the fight," Rodry said, standing tall, taking all of this onto himself. If he weren't so angry at the stupidity of it all, Godwin might almost be proud.

"Well, they'll be stuck taking part in one soon enough," he said. "Do you think a man like King Ravin won't strike back? I sent his ambassador on his way because he couldn't *do* anything to us. Now you've given him a reason to try harder."

"And we'll be there ready to stop him when he does," Rodry said. Of course he was unrepentant. He might be a man grown, and a knight, but he had never known true war. Oh, he'd fought with bandits and creatures, as any Knight of the Spur would, but he hadn't faced a full army on the battlefield the way Godwin had in his youth, hadn't seen the chaos, and the death, and the...

"Enough," Godwin said. "You were a fool to do this, Rodry. You must learn better if you're ever to be worthy to be king."

"I–" Rodry began, clearly ready to argue.

"Be quiet," Godwin said. "You want to argue because your temper won't let you do anything else. Well, I'm still king, and I don't want to hear it."

For a moment, he thought that his son might argue anyway, and then Godwin would have to find a punishment that would actually stick when it came to the heir to his throne. Thankfully, Rodry held his tongue.

"If you ever do something as stupid as this again, I'll have your status as a knight taken from you as a disgrace," Godwin said. It was the worst thing he could think of when it came to Rodry, and the message of it certainly seemed to hit home. "For now, step back out of my sight, before I lose my temper the way *you* always seem to."

He could see Rodry reddening, and he thought that his son might stay and argue, but he seemed to think better of it. Instead, he turned on his heel and stalked from the hall. Maybe he *was* capable of learning something after all. He sat back on a throne made of hard, dark, unyielding wood, waiting to see who would come forward next, if anyone would dare, given that he still had anger lingering after rebuking his son.

Finnal, his soon to be son-in-law, filled the void, stepping forward smoothly and giving a bow that was even smoother.

"Your majesty," he said. "Forgive me, but given how disrupted things have been with the wedding preparations, my family feels that I should make one or two... requests."

His family, which meant Duke Viris, who still stood there smiling in the background, calm as a heron standing above a river waiting to see what he could grab. He was a man who never seemed to be directly responsible for anything, but always seemed to just *be* there, slightly out of reach of any blame.

"What requests?" Godwin asked.

Finnal stepped forward to hand him a rolled length of parchment. Even that was well done, because it meant that he would never have to read out the demands within the parchment himself.

They *were* demands; very subtle ones, but demands nonetheless. Where before, the lands offered as a dowry had run to just short of several villages, now, the revised suggestion was that it should include them. There was more money, of course, because inevitably there would be more money, but the real gains of it were hidden away, spread across an extra fishing vessel here, a tithe from a mill there. None of it looked very much, and if Godwin were openly outraged by it, he would probably look like a miser, but when you added it together, it was a definite increase.

"This is not what our families have already agreed," he pointed out.

Finnal offered another of those elegant bows. "My father is a big believer that an agreement can always be ... renegotiated. Besides, that was before other circumstances came to light, my king."

"What other circumstances?" Godwin demanded.

"The risk of scale sickness within a family always makes it harder to marry into," Finnal said. He sounded apologetic about it, but Godwin didn't believe that tone for a moment. Was *this* why his father had stood there and had another noble bring Nerra's sickness into the light? For a *renegotiation*?

Godwin rose from his throne, his anger propelling him. He wasn't sure what he would have said then, what he would have done, but he didn't get any chance to do it, because in that moment the doors to the great hall burst open, letting in a guard who seemed to be all but holding up a serving girl. Godwin normally didn't pay that much attention to the individual servants, but he felt sure that this was one of the ones who had gone off with Lenore, just days before.

The sight of her there was enough to make Godwin stop short, a hand of cold fear wrapping around his heart where before there had been only the heat of anger.

"Your majesty," the guard called out. "Your majesty, there has been an attack!"

It took a second before Godwin could even speak, his fear was so great.

"What kind of attack? What happened?" he demanded. He looked over to the young woman there, who looked as though she was barely standing.

"We ... we were ..." She shook her head as though she could barely even bring herself to say it. "There was an inn ... there were people there. King Ravin's people ..."

Now the fear inside Godwin gave way to horror.

"Lenore, where is she? Where *is* she?" he demanded.

"They took her," the servant said. "They killed the guards, and they took us, and they ..." The pause told Godwin everything he needed to know. "They let some of us go, they *wanted* us to tell you."

"And Lenore?" Godwin asked. "What about my daughter?"

"They still have her," the young woman said. "They said they were going to take her south, over the bridge. They're going to give her to King Ravin."

In that moment, nothing else mattered; not his son's overreactions, not his son-to-be's demands. All that mattered was the thought that another of his daughters was in danger, and this time, he wasn't going to fail her, not like he had with Nerra.

"Summon my knights!" he called out. "Send messages to the Knights of the Spur. Summon my guards. I want every man we have gathered together! Why are you standing there? Move!"

Around him, guards and servants broke into motion, some running to send messages, some hurrying to go get weapons. For his part, Godwin stalked from the hall, heading through the castle, not caring how many followed him. He all but ran down a spiral stair, feet rattling off the well-worn stone. He passed along tapestry-lined corridors, along paths that had been worn deep into the tiled floors by generations of feet. He headed down to the armory, where a huge door of solid brass stood between the world and the weapons that the castle held, the finest work that the House of Weapons had. The guards there stepped aside to let him pass.

His armor sat on its stand, breastplate dulled with age, greaves worked with interlocking swirls. Ordinarily, Godwin would have waited for a page to help him, but now he threw it on, fastening buckles, tying stays. He knew he *should* be making his way to the queen's chambers, going to tell her that another of her daughters was in danger. Right then, Godwin could have faced a thousand armies, but he couldn't face doing *that.*

What he was about to face was bad enough. Lenore was in danger, had probably faced horrors that were almost beyond imagining. Even with all his armies, Godwin didn't know if they would be in time to retrieve her, or what foes they would face in the attempt. All he knew was that he couldn't face losing another daughter, not now.

"I will get her back," he said aloud. "Whatever it takes, I will get my daughter *back*."

Chapter Three

Rodry was furious, his anger bubbling up in him the way lava might have bubbled in one of the volcanoes of the far north, hinting at worse to come. Servants rushed past him, and Rodry had to move himself carefully out of their path; he wasn't like his brother Vars, wasn't the kind of man who would take his frustrations out on another.

Frustrations? That wasn't the right word when his father had just humiliated him for doing something that *he* should have done in the first place.

A group of his friends were approaching now, and Rodry waited for them. None of them were yet the knights they wanted to be, but at least he could depend on them to support him.

"Your father seems angry," one of his friends, Kay, said. He sounded nervous about the whole thing.

"You're just nervous because you're the one who escorted the ambassador down to the border," Mautlice said. He was the son of an earl, always good to have on a hunt, and strong with it.

"I won't let him do anything to hurt all of you," Rodry said. "I've already told him that it was down to me alone."

"There was no need," Seris said. He was plump and dressed in layers of velvet, always quick with a quip, but just as quick to back Rodry up.

"I appreciate that," Rodry said. "I have two brothers who will happily dance around what they really want to say. I value people who say what they feel."

"You seem pretty angry about all this," Kay said.

That wasn't a big enough word for what Rodry was feeling now. Humiliated, maybe. Frustrated that he couldn't seem to do the right thing.

Frustrated with his father, who had already sent Nerra away, who seemed to be angry with *him* even though he'd done the only honorable thing when it came to the ambassador, and who seemed to be determined to pander to Finnal and his family, in spite of the rumors about him.

There were days when Rodry was convinced that he would never understand politics. Why should he *have* to, though? A man should do the right thing, the honorable thing, and trust that those around him would do the same. He should be strong enough to protect his friends and strike down evil. Everything else was ... was just playing games.

He headed in the direction of his rooms, through the maze of corridors that filled the castle, the others following in his wake. They headed up along a gallery of stained windows, each twisting the light in a different way, then through a broad receiving room filled with deep oak furniture. Rodry shoved a table aside and kept moving.

Around him, the castle was abuzz, but Rodry was angry enough to ignore that. It was probably just something to do with the wedding. Ever since his father had sent the wedding harvest off early, the castle had been scrambling to keep up.

Rodry made it to his rooms. They were more starkly functional than those of his brothers, with trunks and chests along one wall. His armor stood on a stand, spotlessly clean, cared for with all the precision he'd learned among the Knights of the Spur.

Thoughts of the order brought with it thoughts of Erin, since Commander Harr had sent messages to let the court know where she was. Rodry should have guessed that his little sister would head out to the Spur eventually, but he hadn't, simply because it wasn't the kind of thing that girls did.

Perhaps he should be the one to go out there and fetch her back. As a Knight of the Spur, he had the right to enter their fortress home. As Erin's half-brother, he might be able to talk her around, or at least drag her back. At the same time though, Rodry was glad that at least one member of his family could do as they wished.

"We'll go to the House of Weapons," he said to the others. "Spend some time in the training rings there."

"Again?" Kay said. "I'd rather be hunting."

"You all say that you want to be knights someday," Rodry said. "Well, for that, you need to be able to fight better. Maybe enough lessons with Swordmaster Wendros and you'll even beat me."

That would take a *lot* of lessons, but there was no reason not to give them some hope.

"Come on," he said. "It will impress that maid of my sister's you seem to be so sweet on."

"Do you think so?" Kay asked.

"Well, he needs *something* to impress her," Seris said, and the others laughed.

The group of them felt as though it was about to fall into all the familiar joking and camaraderie, not quite that of the *real* knights Rodry spent time with, but close enough for now, and almost enough to keep his anger in check.

Then a servant came running in.

"Your highness," the man said. "I've been sent to find you. It's about Princess Lenore."

Instantly, Rodry spun toward the man. "What about her? What's wrong?"

Just the servant's tone said that *something* was, and whatever it was, it was bad.

"She's been attacked," the servant said. "King Ravin's people are supposed to be taking her south toward one the bridges. The king is gathering all the knights. He has sent messages to the Spur."

"Gathering knights?" Rodry said, springing toward the stand where his armor lay. "And how long will that take?"

Too long, that was the obvious answer. His father was a king, which meant that he would move slowly, gathering assent, gathering troops. Always preparing, never *acting*. Like with the ambassador.

"My father will waste time," Rodry said. "He will let them get away, and if they make it south, he'll say that my sister is lost." He looked over to the servant. "How was Lenore even attacked? Where were Vars and his men?"

"I…no one knows for sure, your highness," the servant said.

Meaning that Vars hadn't been there when he should have been. Anger flashed through Rodry at that, but also guilt. He should have argued more when his father sent Vars to accompany Lenore, should have insisted on guarding her himself. He should have *been* there.

Well, he would be now. Rodry looked around at his friends. They were not the Knights of the Spur, but they had been on enough hunts, trained with weapons enough times. They were here, and they were all he had.

"Seris, find the others, as many as you can, and as quickly. Tell them what has happened, and tell them that I need them. Mautlice, get us horses waiting. Bribe the stable hands if you have to. Kay, get together the weapons."

"We're joining your father's forces?" Kay asked.

Rodry couldn't contain his anger then. He struck the wall beside him, and the others flinched back.

"My father won't be *fast enough*!" he shouted. "A small group can move faster. No, I'm doing this myself. I'm going to go and get my sister back, and get her *safe*. Kay, if that girl you like is one of her servants, she'll be in danger too. Don't you want to help?"

"I..." Kay nodded.

"All of you," Rodry said. "You say you want to be knights. You say you want to prove yourselves. This is how you do it. We do the things that only knights can do. We protect those who need protecting." He looked at them, imploring them. "Please. I'm asking this not as your prince, but as your friend. Help me save my sister."

There was no reason for them to, of course. They *should* go to his father's forces, should wait to take action along with the rest. Instead, Rodry felt relief as they nodded, one by one.

"I'll find more people," Seris promised. "I think I saw a few down in the long gallery earlier. Maybe a few guards, or knights..."

"Halfin and Twell might come," Rodry said. "But the knights owe their first loyalty to my father." He paused. "I'll not pretend that this is safe. Even if we succeed, my father might still be angry with us for what we do. But I have to do this. I can't stand by."

The others nodded.

"Here, let me help you with your armor," Kay said.

Rodry threw on the chain shirt himself, but he needed his friend's help with the straps of the breastplate and the pauldrons. The gorget and the gauntlets came next. Ordinarily, Rodry wouldn't have ridden like this, but he didn't want to get close to his sister's pursuers, only to have to stop and ready his protection.

"We need to hurry," he said. "There's no time to lose."

The others rushed off about the tasks that he'd set them, and Rodry readied his weapons: sword and spear, dagger and mace. He started off through the castle, and servants moved out of his way. Perhaps they sensed the anger that still boiled inside him, pushing him forward.

By the time he got down to the stables, Mautlice had already succeeded in gathering horses for them. More of his friends were already gathering round, along with half a dozen guards, so that there were perhaps twenty in their company in total. Some of them were as armored as Rodry, but others wore only light leathers or chain, as if they'd thrown on whatever they could find close at hand. Would it be enough?

It would have to be, because there was no time for more. They had to get to Lenore.

Rodry's own horse was at the head of the line. He put a foot in the stirrup and swung himself into the saddle. The gates of the castle were open ahead, showing a view down into Royalsport.

Rodry looked back at his group of men. For a moment, there in the sun, they looked as though they might actually be knights. He didn't know how they would fare against the kind of soldiers King Ravin sent, but he had to hope that they could be fast enough, could *do* enough, to save his sister. He drew his sword, then gestured forward with it.

"Onward!"

As the wedge of their horses rumbled into galloping motion, Rodry just hoped that they would be in time.

Chapter Four

Devin staggered back toward Royalsport, still not quite able to believe what he'd seen, what he'd *found.* How could he have spotted a *dragon,* when they had not been seen in so very long?

It was more than that, though; right then, he wasn't even sure who he was. The dreams that had come to him had hinted that he was someone else, someone from a strange place that wasn't the Northern Kingdom. Devin didn't know what to think of that, didn't know who he was meant to be. Where did what he'd done against the wolves fit into it all, too? He'd done magic, but what did that *mean*?

As he reached the city, his feet turned automatically on the route that would take him over the city's many bridges, toward home. He'd gone a dozen steps through the crowds of the city before he realized that he didn't have a home to go to, not anymore. He couldn't go back to the House of Weapons either, because he didn't work there anymore, so what did that leave?

He looked out over the city, caught in the mid-morning sun that made it seem as though the mists of the day before had never happened. Its thatched houses spread out between the streams that filled the city the way spider-web cracks might spread across a mirror. Devin could make out the districts, noble, then poor, then poorer, down to the spot where Devin's home sat…his *former* home, he corrected himself.

The people there bustled along cobbled streets, toward the businesses in which they worked, or toward the great forms of the Houses that stood over the city. The House of Weapons was already belching smoke from its forges into the sky, while the House of Scholars sat aloof from the cacophony of the city. The House of Merchants squatted at their heart of the city's markets, while the House of Sighs was quiet during the day, the last of the patrons from the night before already gone. The smell of the city was a mixture of smoke and sweat, the press of people impossible to ignore.

Devin looked past all of that, toward the solid, gray-walled block of the castle. Rodry would be there, and the prince might help him. Master Grey might be there, and *this* time Devin might be able to get answers from him. Were Princess Lenore not off on her wedding harvest, there might have been a chance to catch a glimpse of her, and the thought of that made Devin's heart ache even though he knew he should ignore that feeling.

He set off for the castle, his slender form weaving through the crowds on the streets. Being taller than most people, he could pick his route easily enough, steering clear of the stalls that lined the side of the thoroughfares, where the press was thickest, and looking on toward the network of streams that crisscrossed the city. Devin brushed dark hair out of his eyes, wondering if the streams would be low enough at this hour to wade. He thought better of it; even if the fine clothes he'd borrowed from Sir Halfin now had mud on them from the forest, it seemed better not to encrust them with more. At least, not if he wanted to get into the castle.

Devin took the bridges instead, hurrying over one stone and wood span after another, rising up toward the castle. On another bridge, he saw a small troop of horsemen charging their way through the city, clearly in a hurry. Devin thought he caught a glimpse of Rodry at their head, but they were too far away for him to call to.

Instead, he kept going for the castle, making his way up through the wealthier districts of the city. He was used to guards giving him glances as he passed, but now it seemed that they were distracted by something. That was enough to make Devin move faster, since it seemed obvious that whatever had happened, the castle was the best chance for him to find answers.

He reached the gates of the castle and stopped in shock, because of the figure standing there. Master Grey stood in robes of white and gold, worked with mystic sigils and runes that caught the light as he moved to stare straight at Devin. He pushed back his hood, revealing his shaven head and piercing eyes.

"What's happening?" Devin asked. "Why are people rushing around here?"

"That is not what you came here to ask about," Master Grey said, in a tone that suggested he knew *exactly* what Devin had seen.

"No," Devin admitted. "I… I was following you, and then I saw… there was a *dragon*…"

"You want answers," Master Grey said. "You want to know about magic."

Devin nodded.

"How badly?" the sorcerer asked. "Do you really want to know about something that might consume you utterly?"

Devin paused. A day or two ago, and he might have walked away at that thought. Now though… now he had nothing left to lose. No home, no family…

"I want to know," he said.

"Come with me," Master Grey said, turning and walking as if it were settled that Devin would follow. For once, he didn't seem to be disappearing out of view, and Devin was so grateful for the chance to actually keep up with him that he hurried to do so, falling into step with the sorcerer as Master Grey led the way into the castle. Crowds of servants parted, moving aside for the magus.

"I… I dreamed strange things," Devin said as he walked. "I dreamed that I wasn't who I had always thought I was."

Master Grey didn't answer, just kept walking to a set of stairs heading down into the bowels of the castle. There were torches flickering there, casting shadows on stones that seemed older than the rest of the castle, smooth edged, with a hint of the mortar that held them crumbling through time.

"We're heading down," Devin said. "Where are we going?"

Again, he got no answer from the magus. Devin could feel frustration building within him. He stepped in front of Master Grey, determined to get some kind of reaction from him. The sorcerer stopped, looking at him until the uncomfortable weight of his gaze made Devin step aside.

"I just want some answers!" Devin insisted.

"Answers are often valuable," Master Grey said. "But they are rarely just given to us."

"I just want to make sense of the things that I saw," Devin said. "I know I was born on the dragon moon. I know my parents aren't my parents."

"Dangerous things to say," Master Grey said. "Maybe even dangerous things to know."

"And you're not going to explain any of it," Devin guessed. "Why did you even meet me at the gate if you're not going to explain things?"

"Because you have a task to perform," Master Grey said. "One that may prove important in the days to come."

"What task?" Devin said.

They reached a door of dark oak, bound with iron, and Master Grey pushed it open, revealing a cavernous space with a vaulted roof, a window above letting in a shaft of light that spread into a bright circle on a floor of black and white tiles. The room had been equipped with a forge, a smelter, an anvil, and what seemed to Devin like every tool anyone could ever need to work with metal, arranged on racks of blackened iron.

That part was strange enough, but there were symbols worked into every surface, symbols that reminded Devin of those on Master Grey's robes.

"You've put magic into all this?" he asked.

To his surprise, Master Grey shook his head. "This is not to bring magic into this, but to contain it when *you* use it."

"And how do I do that?" Devin said.

Even Master Grey's smile was enigmatic, impossible to decipher fully. "You already know what summoning magic feels like. You just need to guide it into the metal as you work."

"And how do I do *that*?" Devin repeated.

"You will learn," Master Grey assured him. He gestured to the forge. "You will need to, because star metal will not respond just to heat or the hammer."

Devin looked over to where the star metal ore sat waiting by the smelter. He walked over to it, touching it, feeling the sensation of something running from him to it; something he couldn't place, still didn't fully understand.

"It responds to you," Master Grey said. He moved to stand by the wall. "Now you need to *control* that response. Magic is dangerous. My spells will contain it, but were you to get this badly wrong…the metal might consume you."

"Consume me?" Devin repeated. Iron and steel felt a long way away, suddenly.

"The metal soaks in magic. It needs it to shape it, but pour too much in, and you might lose yourself," Master Grey said. "Find your magic, boy. Channel it; use it to shape the metal as you work it. Start the smelter."

Devin wanted to argue, but this was the task that had been set for him. He needed to do this if he was going to earn his place within the castle. He needed to hand the sword to the king... or to Rodry. Either way, he would need to craft it first.

He built up the fire for the smelter, wood first, then charcoal, pumping the bellows, building the heat. He watched the flames, waiting for them to be the correct color to tell him that they were hot enough.

"More than heat, boy," Master Grey reminded him.

Devin reached inside himself, trying to find the power that had come out so readily in the valley. It had responded to the metal, so Devin touched a piece of the ore, concentrating on that feeling. He could feel it, he could *feel* it. He tried to push that feeling into the smelter, into the flames...

He barely threw himself flat in time as flames leapt from it, scorching past him in a way that brought back the vision he'd had of the dragon. Even as he struck the flagstones of the floor, Devin saw the protections Master Grey had woven flare into life to absorb the unleashed power.

"I..." Devin stood on unsteady legs. "I can't do this."

"You can, and you will. Patience."

Devin wasn't feeling patient right then, especially not when he could hear the sounds of people shouting in the castle beyond, almost as loud as if the place were under attack.

"What is going on out there?" Devin asked.

"That is not relevant to your part in this," Master Grey said.

"I want to know," Devin said. He stood back. "What are you keeping from me?"

"There are many things I know that you do not," Master Grey pointed out.

Devin started toward the door. "I'll find out myself."

"Princess Lenore has been taken by King Ravin's men," Master Grey said, in tones that held sympathy, but of a detached kind, as if none of this truly touched him. "Prince Rodry has already ridden to rescue her, while her father is gathering men to march on the bridges to the south."

Devin felt as though his heart had stopped in his chest in that instant. Lenore was in danger? Just the thought of it was enough to make him want to go rushing after her, ready to save her. He didn't know where the feeling came from, but it *was* there, and he knew that he couldn't stand by while she was in danger.

"I need to go join the king's forces," he said, starting for the door again.

Master Grey moved in front of him. "And do what?"

"I could... I could help fight to get her back."

"And do you think there aren't enough men rushing to do that?" Master Grey replied. "Prince Rodry has his... friends. The king has his knights and his guards. You can do nothing by going with them except bring death upon yourself."

He made it sound as certain as a stone falling from a cliff.

"What do you care?" Devin demanded.

"I care because you are too *important* to throw away like this. The boy born on the dragon moon? The one from the prophecy? No, *this* is your role: to learn, to grow into your magic, to forge the sword."

Devin started toward the door again, but Master Grey raised a hand.

"Do you think that the king will not leave you behind if I ask it?" he said. He nodded to the smelter. "Now, you have a task to perform. *Gently* this time."

Devin wanted to argue more, but he knew it would do no good. He wanted to help save Lenore, but Master Grey was frustratingly, impossibly right. He *couldn't* add anything to the men already riding to the rescue, couldn't be the noble warrior who saved her. This was all he could do.

He went back to the smelter, ready to try again. He could feel the frustration inside him, and not just at this. He had so many questions, and Master Grey would never answer any of them.

He would find a way to get answers though, to everything.

Chapter Five

Prince Greave was not used to ships in anything but the theoretical sense. Oh, he had read parts of Samir's *On Navigation* and Hussard's *Around the Coasts* in preparation for the voyage, but neither of them had prepared him for the reality of a violently bucking sea, a crew of sailors who more or less ignored him, and a sky that seemed just one step short of a storm.

The *Serpentine* was a large, three-masted ship, high sided and curved so that it was like a sword cutting through the waves. Small boats sat at the side, lashed up against railings. The sailors were tough-looking men in loose, rough clothes that let them move smoothly around the ship's rigging. They were tough and weathered, nothing like Greave, and they looked at his smooth skin and almost feminine looks with contempt.

Only the thought of Nerra, and what they were going to do to help her, made any of this worthwhile. This was the fastest way to Astare and the great library that lay there. It was the only way to get to a place where he might find a cure for the scale sickness quickly enough. Even then... even then, Greave was worried that he might be too late.

"Is this... normal?" Aurelle asked beside him.

"Starting to wish that you hadn't come?" Greave asked.

She shook her head. "You are here, and so I will be here."

She made it seem utterly natural, yet Greave couldn't imagine another woman following him here, onto the rough seas that had claimed so many lives, on a boat that could be torn apart if it strayed too close to the tearing currents near the banks of the Slate. No other woman had wanted to, but Aurelle was more than just another woman.

"You look queasy," Aurelle said.

Greave dreaded to think how he must look then. Ordinarily, he was slender, with almost feminine features, hair falling in soft waves, features locked in an expression that might have seemed like an artist's perfect inspiration for sadness. Now, his hair was matted with sea salt, and he had the first beginnings of a dark beard dotting his chin. His wasn't a face that could take a beard, even when he wasn't half green with seasickness.

As for Aurelle ... she was perfect.

It wasn't just that she was beautiful, although she was, her skin alabaster, her cheekbones and lips merely the brightest stars among a constellation of perfect features. Her body ... Greave could write poems about her, especially since she was no longer dressed in a courtly gown, but in traveling clothes of gray and silver tunic, corset and britches.

None of that was as important as the fact that she was here, with him, on the best route they could find to Astare's great library. She'd come with him on this hunt to find a cure for the scale sickness when no one else would have, searching to help Nerra, getting on the boat with him willingly, if not entirely happily.

"We couldn't have ridden there?" she asked.

"It's about as far north and east as you can go in the Northern Kingdom without hitting the volcanic lands," Greave said. "To get there riding would be difficult, even dangerous, if it were just the two of us."

"And this isn't?" Aurelle asked, with a gesture toward the sea around them.

There was no sign of land from here; the ships had to travel wide to avoid the risk of dangerous currents near the coast. It was unnerving, when Greave had spent most of his life in the confines of libraries, but at the same time he could feel something in him expanding at the sight of all this. *This* was what the writers he admired had seen, the world in all its glory.

"Greave," Aurelle said, pointing. "Look, a whale."

Greave looked and saw a broad gray shape rising from the water, but the maw at the front was too long and too full of spiked teeth for any whale. Its body was as large as any whale's, but it ran with fronds of flesh that might be mistaken at a distance for seaweed. Greave found his memory flickering back to Lolland's *Creatures of the Deep*, and fear rose inside him.

"That's no whale," he said. "Hold onto something, Aurelle." Louder, he called out so that the crew could hear. "Darkmaw!"

The crew looked round at that, and it took them a second longer to respond than they should have simply because it was him bellowing it rather than one of their own. Greave knew what they must be thinking in that moment: that this was a soft, cosseted prince who wouldn't know a darkmaw from a shoal of herring. Even so, a second later, they saw it for themselves, and they ran for the ship's stock of harpoons.

By that point, the creature was already diving.

Greave watched its shadow through the water, his eyes picking it out as he clung to one of the ropes of the ship. Around him, sailors watched warily, several still scrambling for weapons.

Then the creature struck.

It slammed against the side of the boat, but the boson was already turning the ship away from it, so that it didn't bear the full brunt of the attack. Even so, it was enough to make the ship rock violently, listing to the side strongly enough that only Greave's grip on the rope kept him upright.

Aurelle wasn't so lucky. She cried out as she fell, sliding down toward the edge of the ship. The darkmaw was already rising up, its great mouth open to take its prey while those great fronds clung to the ship, holding it at its tilted angle.

Greave leapt forward on instinct, grabbing for Aurelle, even though it meant letting go of his own safe hold. He felt his fingers fasten onto her wrist, but even as he did so, he could feel his own footing giving way.

Ahead of him, Greave could see harpoons starting to sprout from the creature's flesh, but they didn't seem to make any difference to it. He was sliding closer now, and he could see great, unblinking eyes on him, looking at him with a malevolence that was terrifying.

"Your highness!" one of the sailors yelled, and Greave looked over his way just in time to see the man throw a harpoon to him. The weapon hung in the air for a second before slamming into Greave's palm as he caught it.

"Greave!" Aurelle cried out. She was almost to the edge of the boat now, slowed by Greave's grip on her wrist, but only just. Greave held the harpoon, regretting that he hadn't spent more time training with weapons, knowing that he would have to be close to that great eye before...

He threw the harpoon, and it flew truer than Greave could have hoped. It slammed into the open orb of the darkmaw's eye, plunging deep so that the creature let out a scream that seemed to shake the world. Its bulk reared away from the ship as the vessel started to right itself, the splash as it reentered the water sending a wave over the ship that threatened to swamp it.

Greave clung to Aurelle throughout, determined not to let her go. He pulled her up, holding her to him so that there would be no danger of her falling into the water, but also because he wanted to prove to himself that she was still real, still there, still safe.

"I thought I was going to lose you," he said.

"You saved me," she replied. "I… I don't know what to say…"

"I do," Greave said. He kissed her then, gently. "I love you."

"I… I love you too."

⚜ ⚜ ⚜

Aurelle said the words automatically, because in the House of Sighs, they had taught her well that such things were a tool to be used, just one more way to control the feelings of those who heard them. For those whose only role was to give themselves to others, they were words that could take away an edge of harshness or win more coin. For those like her, they could be a weapon as sharp as any knife.

She *could* have stabbed Prince Greave in that moment. He was close enough, and maybe in the aftermath of the chaos, the sailors there would assume that the beast had done him some harm.

Maybe they wouldn't, though. Maybe they would see what she had done, and kill her for it. Maybe they would assume that the wound was from the creature, but that would still leave her as a woman alone on a boat full of sailors, with no way home beyond their grace.

No, a boat was not the best place to kill the prince, even if her patron would probably tell her to do it now, whatever the risk. Aurelle found herself thinking of Duke Viris and the things he had her do. There was no reason to think that he had any concern for her. His time with her in the House of Sighs had proved that.

Aurelle told herself that she was only being practical, yet there was more to it than that. Greave was a gentle, kind, thoughtful man, who was nothing like most of those Aurelle had met. He had leapt to save her without a moment's thought, throwing himself into danger when he could have just clung to his line and waited for the sailors to drive off the darkmaw. She couldn't imagine Duke Viris doing that.

His mission for her remained: Aurelle was meant to prevent Greave from finding any way to help his sister. She was to distract him, control him, and, if necessary, kill him. Now, Aurelle found herself dreading that necessity, because she didn't know what she would do. She couldn't imagine herself killing Greave, couldn't imagine herself hurting him.

It occurred to her then that not being able to help his sister would hurt him almost as much. Could she really do that? *Should* she do that? Common sense said that she must; that Duke Viris was not just her employer, but the one whose side was likely to be ascendant after all of this. Aurelle had felt what it meant to be at the mercy of powerful men; she had no wish to have one of the most powerful of all angry with her.

And yet... she still clung to Greave, still held this strange, beautiful man who would travel the length of a kingdom to help his sister, who valued books more than violence.

"I love you," she repeated, and reflected that sometimes a dagger could have two edges, and it was as easy to cut oneself with it as an enemy.

They would make land soon enough, and after that... after that she would have to choose.

Chapter Six

Prince Vars rode at the head of his men, trying to stay upright in the saddle and look every inch the royalty he was. He'd always been good at that. He wasn't quite as muscled as Rodry, didn't have the almost feminine beauty of Greave, but he was still young, still handsome, still noble looking in his armor and finery as he rode.

He knew that the guards with him were watching, waiting for his orders. He considered the inn where they'd stayed the night, wrung dry of ale, and meat, and women. Vars had paid for his share of all three, and now the temptation was to just dive back in there.

"Your highness," the men's sergeant said. "Shouldn't we be making time if we're to catch up with the princess on her wedding harvest?"

"*I* give the commands, Sergeant," Vars reminded him, but the irritating thing was that the man had a point. Slacking off for a night had done no harm, and would serve to remind everyone that *he* was the important one. Even so, he knew how angry his father would be if he found out that Vars wasn't there, and Vars had no wish to truly risk his father's wrath.

"Very well," he said. "We march!"

They set off, the sun just getting higher, the warmth pleasant rather than oppressive. They spent the morning making their way back to the crossroads where Vars had chosen for them to go the other way. They rode through open farmland, where fields of wheat and whatever other crops peasants were meant to grow stood on either side. The roads out here were dirt things, with dry stone walls to either side and occasional trees: apple and cedar, oak and pear. A few sheep flocked in one of the fields nearby, stupid as people often seemed to be.

His men, at least, were sensible: when they reached the spot where the fallen crossroads sign lay, they didn't say a word about having been there before. Vars led the way down the other fork; it shouldn't be more than about an hour's ride from there to reach the inn where Lenore was supposed to be spending the night.

After that time alone, just afraid enough of the dangers of the road, she would greet Vars the way she always greeted their hero brother, Rodry. Of course, Vars would still need to spend another few days with her on this journey, trudging around the backwaters of the kingdom to collect tribute, but maybe that didn't have to be so bad now. Maybe some of that tribute could find its way into his coffers along the way...

That pleasant thought kept Vars going while his troops marched in step, heading along the road to the inn. He could see it there in the distance, the buildings visible now through the trees. Vars heeled his horse forward. They would arrive as a single, shining cohort, with Vars at their head...

Something was wrong. There should have been smoke from cooking fires there, should have been a dozen other signs of life. Instead, it was quiet. A part of Vars screamed at him to turn back, to stay away. He knew, though, that doing so would make him look weak, would get back to his father...

So instead he hung back just enough to let the others arrive in the inn before him. From behind the wall of his men, Vars saw the spot where Lenore's carriage had been left, and that made hope rise in him. Then he saw the bodies, and hope fell away again, replaced by a crushing fear.

They lay where they had fallen, or been dragged. Vars recognized the uniforms of the few guards Lenore had taken with her, covered in blood. There were maidservants, too, killed with at least as much savagery, although perhaps not so much speed. Vars's practiced eye knew marks made with careful violence all too well.

Fear filled him then. Some of it was fear for his half-sister, because in spite of what some people thought, Vars was not a monster. Admittedly, more of it was fear for himself, and how their father would react if he found out that Vars had lost Lenore, but that wasn't the *point.*

The point…the point was that this had happened and Vars hadn't been here.

His first thought was relief, because being here would have meant senseless danger, maybe even death, looking at the ease with which it seemed that they'd slaughtered the few guards that had gone with Lenore.

His next thought was that he was *meant* to be there, and that everyone would know it. They would look at him like he was nothing, less than nothing, even though he was a prince of the realm.

"Find my sister!" Vars commanded. "Find out what happened here!"

He sat there atop his horse while his men spread out, watching as they moved from building to building. Vars sat with his hand on the hilt of his sword, not knowing what he would do if attackers were to leap from the buildings around. Would he strike out at them, or sit there frozen, or flee? Certainly, he wasn't going to go into the buildings first, seeking *out* danger.

A part of Vars hated himself for that.

"There's someone here!" the sergeant called out from over by the inn's stables. "She's alive, barely!"

That was enough to send Vars down from his horse, hoping against hope that it was Lenore. If she was dead among all of this…

He burst into the stables and found the sergeant helping a young woman to her feet. She wasn't Lenore, didn't even look like one of her maids. Instead, she wore simple clothes that marked her out as a peasant of some sort, perhaps a servant at the inn. Vars strode up to her.

"What happened here?" he demanded. "Where is my sister?"

The young woman cried out at the violence of his tone, and only the sergeant's soothing grip on her stopped her from pulling away completely. Vars had no time for that. He needed to know what had happened here, needed to know just how much trouble he was in.

"What *happened* here?" he demanded. "Where is Princess Lenore?"

"Gone," the servant said. "The Quiet Men…they took her…"

"Quiet Men?" Vars said, unwilling to believe it. He'd heard the stories. King Ravin's trained killers, taught to cross the bridges to do his bidding.

"They…they killed most of us," the woman said. "They took over the inn, kept only a few of us for…for…"

Another man might have said something soothing in that moment. Vars just watched her.

"Where is my sister?" he repeated.

"They took her," the servant said. "They waited until she came into the inn with her men, and they killed the men, and... they captured her; her and her maids. They kept her here, hurt her, and now they're riding for the South."

"And they left you alive to tell us this?" Vars asked, not entirely believing it. When one did evil things, it was better to do them in secret, away from prying eyes. He knew that as well as anyone.

"They *wanted* people to know," the young woman said. "They killed some of the maids, but others... they sent them out with the news. They left *me* here. They want people to know what they did, that they could get to the princess even here. That they *have* her."

Vars let out a shout that was pure frustration and anger. Those around must have taken it for anger that his sister had been captured like that, that she was in danger. It was more than that, though, so much more. It was the fact that others knew what had happened here, thanks to those the Quiet Men had let go. It was the frustration that others would, inevitably, know about his failure.

It was the understanding of what he would need to do next.

"How many of them are there?" he demanded.

"A... maybe a dozen," the woman said.

A dozen had done all of this? Still, at least there was one advantage to that: they outnumbered them. Vars *liked* it when he outnumbered his opponents.

"Gather the men," Vars snapped.

"What about this one?" the sergeant asked, with a nod to the woman who'd been left.

"My sister's the one who matters!"

She was the one whose safety would count to their father. Come back with her, and Vars could make up any story he wanted about being delayed on the road, then still be counted as a hero. Come back without...

It wouldn't come to that; Vars wouldn't allow it.

He went to his horse, vaulting into the saddle like some hero out of a song. The irony of it wasn't lost on him as his men gathered, forming up together as precisely as if they'd been commanded by a *real* leader.

Vars drew his sword, which was more than he usually did in a fight. He looked out over the men.

"You, see if there are any horses left in the stables. The rest of you, get ready to march, double time." There were a few murmurs from within the ranks, but Vars silenced them with a glare. "My sister, your princess, is in danger! King Ravin's men are taking her back to the Southern Kingdom, and that means crossing the bridges. If we reach them first, we can still stop them, still save her! Every man here can be a hero!"

They all could, but he would be the biggest hero of all. Save his sister, and men would tell stories of how brave Prince Vars had fought the best that King Ravin could offer. Fail… fail and his father would probably have his head.

Kill a dozen men to stop that? Vars would do that and more.

"Forward!" he yelled, and heeled his horse onward. "We need to get to the bridge in time!"

Chapter Seven

The first surprise for Nerra was that she woke at all. Her eyes flickered open, and she could breathe, her body not threatening to consume her. She sat, and the second surprise was the bed that she sat on. It was a thing of stone, covered in blankets, in what appeared to be a long dormitory of similar beds.

On each of those beds, a figure lay, most of them moaning, many of them so still that it looked as though they were only breaths away from death. Nerra could smell sweat, and a kind of heat that seemed to be bone deep. The figures wore a variety of clothes, as if they'd been brought here from all corners of the world, but here and there Nerra could see a patch of bare skin, marred by black, scale-like lines...

They were like her.

Nerra looked round sharply, trying to make sense of this. When she had passed out, there had been only the forest, and the dragon...

"You're awake."

The man who stood near the door was the third surprise. He had a long, curling beard, into which he seemed to have woven shells, each painted with a different sign. His graying hair was also long, falling to his shoulders. He wore a tunic and britches, frayed here and there through overuse. He was tall and broad shouldered, with features that seemed weatherworn and lined by care.

"Who...who are you?" Nerra asked, standing. "Where am I?"

"You are where you need to be, in the last refuge for those with the dragon sickness," the man said. Nerra frowned at that; in the Northern Kingdom, they called it the scale sickness. Did that mean she wasn't *in* the Northern Kingdom anymore?

"I... I feel..." Nerra began. "I was dying."

"You were," the man agreed, in a voice that seemed too calm for the words. "But we have ways of stabilizing the sickness, for a time."

"But that's incredible," Nerra said. "If people knew... my father is—"

"I know who you are, Princess Nerra," the man said. "I know that you were cast out for what you are, but you are safe here. This is a place where all of those with the sickness can live out the days of humanity they have left. Where we do what we can to extend those days a little."

Nerra frowned at that. "You still haven't told me who you are."

"I am Kleos," the man said. "I am the keeper of this place. I saw your arrival; it is rare for one to be brought directly by a dragon."

Rare, but apparently not so rare as to bring out shock in the man there.

"You're talking as if you've seen dragons before," Nerra said. "Where *is* this?"

"Come," he said. "It is better if you see for yourself."

He led the way out of the dormitory, into a large open space that seemed to be almost like a village. People worked there, tilling small plots of vegetables or carrying water. Each and every one seemed to have the scale mark somewhere on their body.

The land around the village was rocky, rising on slopes that led up to the lip of what looked like a volcano. Other rock formations lay scattered around in basalt, dark and angular, as if grown from the volcano's fire. There were trees on some sections of the slope, growing out of the dark soil, while in the distance, the ground fell away toward the surrounding sea, making the whole place into an island. A jetty down below suggested how most people reached there.

It was what lay beyond that caught Nerra's eye most, though. So far off that it was barely visible on the horizon, she saw a shoreline far larger than that of the island, volcanoes rising up from the landscape to give it a jagged, toothed appearance. Above the volcanoes, here and there, she saw circling dots. It took a moment to realize just how huge they would be, and it was only then that she realized *what* they had to be: dragons.

"That's Sarras," Nerra said in shock. She had never seen the third continent, but there was only one place that it could be. If true though, it meant that her dragon had carried her halfway across an ocean. "I'm on Sarras."

"Not quite," Kleos said, gesturing to the small community around them. "This is Haven. Our island sits quite apart from the horrors of ... that place."

"What horrors?" Nerra asked.

Kleos shook his head. "This is not a place for that. This is a place of peace, where those with the sickness can live out their days, and find a graceful death."

"A ..." Nerra shook her head at that thought. She was supposed to just sit here and wait for death? "What is this place? A prison? Am I supposed to be a captive here?"

"This is a place of refuge," Kleos said. "Where those with the dragon sickness can be safe from the world around them, and the world can be safe from them."

"That's the second time that you've called it that," Nerra pointed out. "Is it just because of the scales?"

"It is because of what people with the sickness become," Kleos said. He paused for a moment. "I ... I could show you, but it might be better not to. There might be more peace in not knowing what awaits."

Nerra didn't hesitate. "Show me."

No one else had been able to truly show her where her disease was going to lead. The physicker had *told* her, but that wasn't the same, not even close. Nerra needed to see it for herself. She followed as Kleos led the way to a different part of the community, to a stone building whose door seemed solider than the rest. He took out a key, unlocking it.

"We must be careful within," he warned. "The ones here ... they have little humanity left."

"But you said that there were ways to help," Nerra said.

"There are," Kleos agreed. "But do not let that lure you into false hope, Princess. There is no cure. Eventually, even with all I do, it leads to this."

He stepped back to let Nerra inside, so that she could see. Inside the building it was shadowy, the darkness cut through by the whimpering and moaning of those within. There was nothing human about this sound, though.

There was certainly nothing human about the creature that rose up in front of her. It was larger than a man, with scaled, clawed hands, teeth that looked as though they could bite straight through flesh, and features that had been distorted into a kind of lizard-like snout. Its body was bulky and misshapen, muscles seeming to grow under the skin in ways that made no sense. Its eyes were human, but there was no humanity left in them, only rage, and pain, and hunger. It was a thing that was no longer human, but wasn't quite a dragon, either, caught somewhere between, unfinished, twisted out of one form but not quite into the next.

It lunged forward at Nerra, and she was too slow to dodge in that moment. The bulk of the creature was on her then, knocking her to the ground and looming over her. Its claws rose up, ready to strike, and Nerra was sure then that Kleos had only brought her there to die at its hands for reasons she couldn't begin to fathom.

Then Kleos was there. He had a wavy blade in his hands that seemed to have been made of some dark metal, the knife as long as Nerra's forearm. He thrust with it, catching the creature in the chest so that it shrieked out in an animal cry. It fell back, claws up as if to ward off more cuts, but Kleos was already advancing.

"I'm sorry," he said, as Nerra started to stand. "When I brought you here I did not know that this one would be quite so far along. It… it is time for him."

"That used to be a person?" Nerra asked. She couldn't believe it, wouldn't believe it, because… that would mean that *she* would end up like that. "Isn't there anything you can do to help?"

"Only one thing now," Kleos said, and stepped forward after the creature. His expression was filled with pity, but even so, it didn't stop him from stepping inside the circle of the dragon-thing's claws. He thrust sharply with the blade he held, this time up under its jaw, up into its brain. Nerra heard the creature give a gasp that seemed part shock, part relief, then Kleos dragged his blade clear, letting the beast slump back to the floor.

He stood there over it for several seconds. From deeper in the building, Nerra could hear growling that suggested more of these things… these *people*, were there.

"Help me to carry him outside," Kleos said. "He has found peace now, and we will treat his body with honor."

Nerra didn't know what to do, so she got a hold of the creature's legs, helping while Kleos lifted.

"Will that..." she began. "Will I..."

"Will you end up like Matteus here?" Kleos asked. He bowed his head. "Some do not live so long. The dragon sickness tears them apart. But yes, you might."

"And when I do, you'll kill me?" Nerra said.

Kleos nodded. "I will give you peace, when there is nothing left in you that knows it."

Nerra felt sick then. Her dragon had brought her here, had saved her, yet now... now it looked as though the only thing it had saved her for was death.

Chapter Eight

Lenore hoped for death as she sat on the horse, her hands bound before her and Ethir's grasp around her waist holding her there firmly. Around them, the other Quiet Men rode, horses moving in a near silent line, those riding them doing so with their hands on the strange assortment of weapons they carried.

Before, she had hoped for escape, but the Quiet Men had shown her twice now that there was no way for her to escape them. They had caught her easily, back in the inn, and captured her again just as smoothly when she had tried to flee. She could not escape.

Then, she had hoped for rescue. Lenore had been certain that it would come, with the Knights of the Spur riding over the horizon, or Rodry, even Vars, coming with the men who should have been guarding her. Here, in the open, couldn't they sweep down on these dozen and defeat them? Couldn't they save her?

Yet with every passing league, those hopes were fading. They got closer to the bridges and further from any help with every stride of the horses. Already, Lenore could see the largest of the bridges in the distance, its span stretching out over the Slate in length after length of dark wood.

There were guards at the end of the bridge, perhaps half a dozen, but as Lenore and the Quiet Men rode forward, she knew they wouldn't stop a force such as this. They were a big enough force to stop smugglers, or to collapse the bridge in the event of an invasion, protecting the kingdom with the fury of the river, not the strength of their numbers. They weren't there to fight a force coming from this side. Most weren't even facing the right way as the Quiet Men descended on them, looking out over the river instead, making sure that no threat was coming from the other side.

She saw some of them turn at the sound of the approaching horses, but they were too late. The first of the Quiet Men were already striking at them, cutting down with swords, striking out with knives. They fell on the guards, and it wasn't even a fight, not really. Most of the men there didn't even manage to draw their swords. Of those who did, more died without ever managing to use them. One managed a clumsy blow aimed at one of the Quiet Men, but the simple truth was that those who guarded the bridges were not the finest of the kingdom's warriors, just those who were prepared to sit there longest, managing the trade between the two sides of the bridge. That guard died as quickly as the others, a spray of blood coming from his throat as one of the Quiet Men opened it with a sword.

Lenore's captors paused there for a moment or two, cleaning their weapons before proceeding. It gave Lenore a chance to look out over the bridge, staring out to the far shore, and the trees there beyond a stretch of open ground. That was ground that did not belong to her father, ground from which she couldn't imagine anyone bringing her back.

"Almost there," Ethir murmured behind her. "King Ravin is going to enjoy breaking you."

Lenore thought of all the things that had happened to her in the day before, and all the things that might still happen. King Ravin was not known for his kindness, and if he had her as his captive... Lenore found herself hoping again for death, because even death would be better than what might follow.

As the horses of the Quiet Men started out over the expanse of the bridge, Lenore found herself looking out over the side, down at the rushing rage of the Slate below. It was a river that no one could hope to swim in, and that could tear apart boats that tried to cross it. Anyone who fell in would be carried away in seconds, and drowned within a minute.

Wouldn't a minute of even that horror be better than everything that was waiting on the other side?

Lenore couldn't believe that she was thinking about this, couldn't believe what she was contemplating. She found herself thinking about her family in that moment, about her father, her mother, her brothers and sisters. She found tears falling down her cheeks at the thought of them, the agony of all that she might lose flooding through her.

Erin would probably have fought her way free by now, while if Rodry were here, he would have cut down half of the Quiet Men to free her. Greave would have come up with some cunning plan out of a poem, and even Nerra might have found some plant along the way to help her, or poison her captors.

Lenore had none of that, only the feel of her captor's arm around her waist, the certainty of the life that would follow if, *when*, she reached the far side of the bridge. She couldn't do it, couldn't let that happen, even though it meant...

"I'm sorry," she whispered, picturing her family, and then she threw herself to one side.

Lenore tumbled from the horse, caught her footing, and then flung herself at the edge of the bridge. She clambered up its side, her bound hands making her progress slower than it should have been. Even so, she managed to make it up there onto the railing that normally kept horses and carts from going over into the water.

Lenore balanced there, looking down, terror filling her even as she knew that this was the only way, the only thing that would keep her from far, far worse. Taking a breath, she stepped off into air.

For a moment, Lenore hung there, tumbling down, plunging toward the water as if she might dive into it headfirst. She held her breath automatically, even though she knew there was no way to swim clear of the torrent, no way to survive what was to come...

Then a hand caught hold of her ankle, grip as unyielding as steel, arresting her fall.

"No you don't, girl," Eoris's voice said. Lenore kicked at his grip, trying to break free, but there was no give to him, no chance even to escape into death. More hands caught hold of her, and Syrelle's voice joined his.

"You think you get to leave us that easily? Let's get you back up."

Lenore struggled, but it didn't make any difference. They dragged her up, pulling her back over the railing of the bridge, depositing her on its boards the way they might have a sack. They hauled Lenore to her feet, and Syrelle stood there a moment before bringing her hand round in a stinging slap.

"Every time you try to break free, we will bring you back," she said. "You will not be allowed to die, and you will be hurt each time you try. Do you understand?"

Through her tears, Lenore managed to nod.

They threw her over another horse, this time flung across the saddle rather than allowed to sit. Lenore couldn't even get down now, with no chance to try to throw herself into the water once more.

When she couldn't even die, what was there left? Lenore lay there and sobbed, knowing that she had no more choices, no more *chances.* She stared at the far bank and wondered if King Ravin was somewhere nearby, or if he would be waiting further back, ready for her to be dragged before him.

Lenore looked back toward the northern bank, thinking of home, thinking of all that she was about to lose. That was why she saw the band of soldiers charging down on horseback, weapons and armor shining in the sunlight.

In that moment, she saw one thing she had never thought that she would see: she saw Vars there at the head of the wedge of men, looking like an avenging angel as he led the charge forward. There, like that, he was every inch the noble knight, riding to the rescue, ready to fight for the safety of his half-sister and bring her back safely to the waiting arms of her family. It was the kind of thing that Lenore associated more with Rodry than with him, but even Vars's presence was enough to make hope well up inside her.

He would come, and he would save her, and...

...and he was stopping, slowing his charge, bringing his knights to a halt. No, he couldn't be doing that. He couldn't just be standing there while the Quiet Men carried her away to a fate worse than death. No brother would do that, would they, even Vars?

Yet he *was* doing it, stopping short in the face of the enemies across the river. He was doing what Vars always did, backing away in the face of danger, and that meant...

...that meant that he wouldn't interfere. They would drag Lenore away to King Ravin, and Vars would do nothing about it.

"No," she sobbed. "No!"

Chapter Nine

Vars burst out into the space before the bridge, feeling the ecstasy that came from a whole unit of men charging in his wake, ready to follow his commands. He knew that, at a single order from him, they would fall on any enemy he chose and kill them without hesitation. *That* was power; and in that moment he thought he understood why Rodry enjoyed his knightly games so much.

Then he saw the bridge ahead, and the party already crossing it. Vars thought he could see Lenore there, making out his half-sister's presence on one of the horses there. For a moment, he thought that he saw her looking back at him in hope, maybe even expectation...

The problem was that, even as Vars watched, they reached the far side of the bridge.

"Hold!" Vars commanded, and the men around him did as he ordered, even though it was obvious that they didn't understand why. They milled about, lined up ready to charge, clearly eager to do it.

"Your highness," the sergeant said. "They're getting away. We need to—"

"*I* decide what we need to do," Vars snapped, hating himself even as he said it. The truth was that a part of him longed to charge down there as much as any of the soldiers did. He wanted to be the one to save his sister, wanted to see his father's gratitude at his bravery.

The problem was that he couldn't.

Vars couldn't bring himself to heel his horse forward, couldn't bring himself to force it over that bridge, couldn't set foot in the south like that. Here... *here* he was safe, but there... there could be soldiers waiting in the trees beyond, could be a whole army hidden just south of the river. To charge to the south was to invite disaster, to expose himself to dangers that seemed to swirl, impossible to know, in the back of his mind.

In a realm that was under his family's control, Vars felt as though he could do anything. *Did* do anything, safe in the knowledge that nobody could touch him. There, though, past the bridge, there was nothing to protect him beyond the strength of his arm and the loyalty of his men. Just the thought of that made Vars feel sick with worry.

"Your highness..." the sergeant began again, but Vars cut him off.

"Be silent! Do you want to start a war? If we cross that bridge, that's what it means: a war! And I... I am the second in line to the throne. What if they're crossing in full view of us to lure me across? What if this is some kind of trap?"

It was an excuse rather than a reason, and Vars knew even as he said it that he hadn't convinced his men. He could see their looks of disapproval, so similar to those he faced back in Royalsport whenever he wouldn't hunt or fight. Someone would pay for those looks, but not now, not now...

At least they could do nothing about it. None of the men dared to disobey Vars, which meant that none of them could show him up. None of them could show his fear for what it was. All of them had to sit there, watching while the small group of enemies passed over the bridge, into the Southern Kingdom and down along the road.

They were just on the edge of sight when the unthinkable happened: a second set of horsemen approached from the north. Even then, it might have been all right; Vars might still have remained in control of the situation, except for one stupid, hateful thing...

Rodry was at their head.

⚜ ⚜ ⚜

Rodry charged, pushing his horse as hard as he could, only holding back at all because if he killed it before he caught up to his sister, he would find himself walking after her to save her. Beside him, his friends pushed their own horses, looking every inch the knights they sought to be, hair streaming in the wind, weapons shining in the sun.

Ahead, he saw a bridge to the south, saw the dot of the group beyond it just disappearing into the landscape beyond. Rodry breathed a sigh of relief at that, because it meant that he'd guessed right about the route they would have to take. If they'd taken one of the smaller crossings, he might never have found his sister, but the sight of her there was enough to spur him on to greater efforts.

Then Rodry saw Vars, saw him standing there with a whole troop of men, simply *watching* their sister be carried away. Anger burned in him at that, and that anger was enough that he didn't just ride past Vars in contempt. He rode to him instead, stopping and gesturing over the bridge.

"What are you doing?" Rodry demanded. "Why aren't you riding after Lenore?"

"If we cross the bridge, it's war," Vars replied, but Rodry could hear the tremor in his voice, guess the real reason for his reticence.

"It's already war!" Rodry roared back at him. "And where were you when our sister was being captured?"

"I was ... we took a wrong turn on the road."

Rodry stared at him, unable to believe it. He *didn't* believe it; Vars was many things, but he wasn't stupid. He could read a map, find his way. If he hadn't caught up with Lenore, it was because he hadn't wanted to.

"What was it?" Rodry demanded. "Did you get distracted by all the inns on the way, or did you just not think that our sister was worth your time to protect? Or were you too scared to play the part of a guard? That was it, wasn't it, Vars? Cowardice, the same as always."

"I'm no coward," Vars insisted.

"Then prove it!" Rodry shouted back at him. "Charge over that bridge and get our sister back."

"I ..." Vars hesitated, and that was all that Rodry needed to know.

"Coward," Rodry said. "Sitting here, trying to save your own skin."

"I'm second in line to the throne!" Vars insisted. "You think I should risk myself for a sister who will never be—"

Rodry hit him then, hard enough to knock Vars sprawling from his saddle. His brother came up, hand going to the hilt of his sword, but one look at Rodry's expression had him stepping back, then scrambling away.

Rodry looked back across the bridge. His sister and her captors were out of sight now; even in this Vars had found a way to make things more difficult. He had no way of knowing which way they would have taken her, where they might be. Even so, he wasn't going to let that stop him.

"We need to ride," he said to the others. "But I've no idea where."

"King Ravin has a hunting lodge in a village a little way south of the border," Kay said, surprising him. "What? My father used to trade with the south. King Ravin used to make a point of receiving visitors as grandly as possible with wine and..."

"And women," Rodry finished for him.

Kay paled at that, then nodded.

It was a possibility, and there would be tracks. Years of hunting had given Rodry practice in that, at least. He looked around at his friends.

"I'll not lie to you," he said. "I hoped to catch up to Lenore before she crossed the border. Going after her now means going into the heart of the enemy's lands. It means more danger for all of us. If any man wishes to turn back..."

None of his friends moved. Rodry had known that they wouldn't, but he had to ask. He turned to the guards who had accompanied Vars, pointedly ignoring his brother.

"You men," he said. "I think that you are not the cowards my brother is. I think you were misled."

One of the men, a sergeant, nodded. "The prince told us we were marching the right way, your highness. Otherwise, we'd have been at the princess's side, defending her."

Rodry believed him. He wanted to believe that no true man would have shirked his duty, given the choice. It only made what Vars had done worse.

"Some of you will have to stay here to report the truth of all this to my father," Rodry said. "I want to make sure that he hears *all* of this. But if any of you will ride with me, I'd be grateful for the help, and so will the kingdom."

"I'll ride with you," the sergeant said.

"And me," a soldier called out.

More calls came from around Rodry, in a chorus of raised voices and stamping feet that seemed to shake the ground around him. He charged for the bridge, and those men with horses charged with him, leaving Vars standing at the heart of a pitifully small group of foot soldiers, all looking at him with some of the contempt that Rodry felt for his brother in that moment.

He felt more than that though. The old, familiar anger was roaring through Rodry now, fueling his galloping race across the boards of the bridge, down into the Southern Kingdom. He *would* get his sister back. He *would* make those who had taken her pay. Anything that got in his way…

…anything that got in his way would burn.

Chapter Ten

King Godwin paced the castle's main courtyard, while around him men rushed back and forth, preparing for war. His every footstep rang with metal as his armor sounded against the stone cobbles of the floor, but it still wasn't enough to drown out the shouting as men issued commands or ran to be in place among the others there.

"Why have you not gone yet?" Aethe demanded by his side. "Why have you not recovered our daughter?"

His wife looked like a wild thing, as far from the woman Godwin had married all those years before as he could imagine. She had torn at her clothes, while there were gouges in her hands from her nails. Godwin could understand that. She was simply as distraught as any mother had a right to be, when all her daughters were missing. That Erin was safe among the Knights of the Spur meant nothing, when Nerra was banished, and Lenore had been taken.

"We will be going soon, my love," Godwin promised.

"I'm not your love," she snapped back. "Not when you've lost all my girls!"

"My men tell me that Rodry has gone after Lenore," Godwin insisted. "They saw him racing off from the city. And Vars ... well, there is no word from Vars, but he should be with her."

"And meanwhile, you sit just *gathering men*," Aethe said. She made that into an insult, turning on her heel and heading off toward the interior of the castle. On another day, Godwin would have gone after her, but not today. Today, he needed to finish gathering his men, and set off in pursuit of Lenore.

"Go with the queen," he said to a pair of his guards. "Make sure that she is safe."

On another day, he might have sent knights to her, but he needed his knights for this. He could do nothing to help Nerra, and by his own laws could not stop Erin from joining the knights, but he could help Lenore, *would* help Lenore.

"How much longer until all is ready?" he demanded, as servants and ostlers rand around the horses, readying them.

"A few minutes more, your majesty," one of the grooms called out. A few minutes? How could he wait any more, when his daughter was in danger the whole time? It was at times like this that Godwin wished that he were like his son Rodry, able to charge off in pursuit of what he felt, unconstrained by the needs of the kingdom.

Instead… instead, Godwin had to do what was right. He understood what this capture of his daughter meant: an open declaration of war by King Ravin. That meant that he could not simply charge down with a few men the way Rodry had done, not when there might be a whole army coming the other way. He had to order preparations, even though every instinct he had screamed at him to simply ride in an attempt to reach Lenore in time.

"Send men to the bridges," Godwin ordered Sir Lars of the Two Swords. "Tell the men there that I have commanded them destroyed."

That would not be a hard task. Each of the bridges had the means to destroy it built in, whether it was oiled slats that would burn, or linchpins that could be pulled away to allow it to collapse. For so long, those had been the kingdom's defense, and they would prove so again.

"*All* the bridges, your majesty?" the knight asked. "If your daughter has passed to the south, and we are to recover her…"

The king in Godwin knew that he should order all of the bridges destroyed. That this might be the point of Ravin's plan, forcing him to leave at least one route an army could cross. Even so, the father in him could not even contemplate that. He could not abandon his daughter like that, or his son, because Godwin had no doubt about how far Rodry would go to recover Lenore.

"You are right, my friend," he said. "Let one bridge stand, one of the minor ones, so that Ravin can't march an army across unless it's two by two, but all others are to fall. If this is the precursor to an invasion, we will force Ravin to come to us where he cannot use his whole army."

That was one part of this that struck Godwin as strange: Ravin was reputed to be a ruthless and cunning king, who had to know how strong the defenses of the bridges were. The North had been safe from the South for generations thanks to the Slate's roaring rapids, and how easy it was to just collapse a bridge beneath an invading force. What did he hope to achieve by doing this now?

"Perhaps he hopes to lure *us* to the attack," Godwin mused. It was the only thing that made sense.

"What's that, your majesty?" Sir Lars asked.

Godwin shook his head. "It doesn't matter, just go. Sir Twell!"

The knight was there, assisting with the preparations, ensuring that all was planned well. Godwin would have expected nothing less. Sir Ursus was beside him, lifting the heaviest of the supplies.

"You and Ursus ride to the Spur. Tell the knights there that there is to be war, and bring them south. We will show Ravin our true strength."

"As you command, my king," the knight said, sweeping a bow and then mounting a horse. How long would it take him and Sir Ursus to bring the other knights? Days, at least. If Ravin did come in force, could they hold until then if they could not collapse the bridge? Would they be able to get Lenore back before anything worse happened?

So many thoughts were swirling around in Godwin's head then. He had forgotten what the build up to conflict felt like, forgotten all the ways that doubts could creep in. Still, at least he had one way to deal with that. Stalking off across the courtyard, he set off in the direction of his wizard's tower.

Of course, he did not get there before Master Grey found him. He was waiting at the second turn of a corridor within the castle, standing there before a statue of one of Godwin's ancestors as if studying it.

"Why are you not out there, helping me prepare for war?" Godwin demanded.

The magus continued to stare at the statue for a moment or two. "Do you know the story of King Lorus?"

"What?" Godwin demanded.

"Your great-great-great grandfather, I believe."

"I know who the man was," Godwin snapped. Why did Master Grey always bring up irrelevancies at times like this? "What about him?"

"He was a man who fought seven times against enemies to the south, allowing them across the bridges so that he could face them," the sorcerer said. "He won each time, and yet, when hot summers brought droughts, he could do nothing."

"What are you saying? That Ravin will find a way to affect the *weather*?" Godwin asked.

The sorcerer gave him one of those looks he seemed to do so well, which said that the king had misunderstood him, or would never manage to see all that he saw, or both.

"I am saying that, sometimes, the conflict we think is important is the smallest of things, compared to all the world might throw our way."

"The South stealing my *daughter* is not *unimportant,*" Godwin snapped back. "Lenore is in danger, and Ravin ... he wouldn't have done this if he didn't plan to be waiting."

"That is one possibility," Master Grey agreed, or was it agreement? It was hard to tell with the man. If he hadn't done so much to assist the kingdom over the years ...

"Why didn't you see this coming?" Godwin demanded. "You're supposed to be the one who can unpick the future. Why didn't you tell me that my daughter was in danger?"

The sorcerer raised his shoulders in a shrug. "My focus was ... elsewhere."

"Then bring it back to where it should be!" Godwin roared at him, and he wasn't sure if he'd ever shouted at his magus like that before. "Read your auguries, look at your stars. Do your *job,* while my daughter is in danger."

If the sorcerer was perturbed by the outburst, he gave no sign of it, but then, he never gave any sign of what he was truly thinking. There were days when Godwin wondered if he was a charlatan, and others when it seemed as if the man might have more power than anyone else alive.

"Not anyone," Master Grey murmured, and that made Godwin pause.

"What did you say?"

The sorcerer seemed to catch himself.

"You wish me to look at the future for you, my king? Very well."

He crouched there, in the hallway, squatting the way a beggar might have in spite of his robes of pristine white and gold. He took a pouch from his belt, drawing out what seemed to be a scattering of knucklebones. To Godwin's surprise, the sorcerer spat on them, quick and sharp. He threw them onto the floor, the rattle of it filling the space. He then took a knife, pricking at his thumb to let a single bead of blood form. Godwin hadn't been entirely sure that Master Grey possessed blood at all. That bead fell onto the knucklebones.

The sorcerer seemed to stare at them for a long time.

"Tell me," Godwin said. "Tell me how to find Lenore."

"I see what I see," Master Grey said. "And I see an ending. A king must fall, and not. He must die so that things might shift."

"You mean me," Godwin said. "You think I'm to die? Tell me who does it. I'll cut him down before he gets close."

The sorcerer smiled thinly. "The hand that wields the blade is not the hand to kill you, King Godwin. We do not always die by the hand that we think..."

Anger rose up in Godwin then. "Damn you, sorcerer," he snapped. "You and your prophecies. I ask you for help finding my daughter, and you give me my death."

He strode back in the direction of the courtyard, then turned to call out over his shoulder.

"Well, I'll surprise you yet. I'll get Lenore back. I'll beat Ravin. And anyone who comes at me with a blade will eat my steel!"

Grey was gone, of course. Only his words remained, ringing in Godwin's ears.

"Not by the hand you think."

Chapter Eleven

Erin rode hard back toward the Spur, ignoring the pain of the knife wound in her leg. She sat tall in the saddle, chain shirt shining, short spear slung across her back. There were still traces of blood in the short darkness of her hair, because there hadn't been time to truly clean up in the aftermath of their fight against the Quiet Men, not when they needed to carry the news back to the fort.

Sir Til and Sir Fenir rode beside her. Fenir was as quiet as always, graying and brooding beneath thick eyebrows, the clink of his half plate the only sound as he rode. It was more of a surprise that Til was just as quiet, riding forward with a fixed determination, his expression drawn and pale.

"You can't still be angry that I charged in back at the village," Erin said. "After everything they'd *done*?"

"And if they'd killed us, no one would know," Til said. "If we didn't make it back, there would still have been Quiet Men there, waiting to strike. Now, hurry your riding. We've a warning to deliver."

Erin knew all of that, understood the consequences, but still wasn't about to let it go. The Quiet Men had murdered an entire village's worth of people. They deserved to die. She could no more have walked away and left them in peace than she could have knelt before them and let them cut her throat.

"Leave her be," Fenir said. "We need to focus on getting back."

Erin heard Sir Til sigh. "True. And you did fight well. You're getting good with that spear. You'll need to be."

Erin knew why: war was coming. The Quiet Men taking a village was just the start. If they'd done that here, how many other places had they done it? How many more enemies would be coming?

It didn't matter. They would kill them, no matter how many there were.

It was a long ride back to the black, jutting rock of the Spur. By the time it came into view, Erin could feel the ache of her muscles, the pain of her carefully bound wound growing with the effort of riding. Erin ignored it, because she was not some sensitive princess who needed to stop because of a little pain. She was a warrior, and she would be a knight.

Eventually, the fortress rose up ahead of them, sticking out on a random jutting of glassy black rock left over from the wars that had divided the continents. Gray stone stood above it, the gates open now to welcome them back.

As Erin and the others rode in, horns blared in welcome, and knights stood to either side in welcoming lines, swords raised. Erin felt like a returning hero, welcomed back into the embrace of a group of warriors out of stories, each one as powerful a fighter as any she'd met.

Beyond those ranks, she was surprised to see that the knights were starting to gather in the main yard of the fort, moving with an urgency that she didn't normally associate with their training. Commander Harr stood at the heart of it all, gray-haired and bearish, his authority obvious as he called out commands.

"Every man is to bring rations for a month. The king might think this will be over soon, but King Ravin is a dangerous foe."

He turned as Erin and the others approached. Erin slid down from her horse, hiding her wince of pain as her feet hit the ground.

"You're back, good, just in time," he said. "Tell me how your patrol went."

Erin tensed then. Sir Til had been clear that he disapproved of how she'd handled things back at the village. What if Commander Harr agreed? What if this was all that he needed in order to send her back to be married off to whoever her parents could find for her?

"We found a group of Quiet Men holed up in a village," Sir Til said. "They'd taken the whole thing, killing the villagers."

"Forming a base," Fenir added, in his usual clipped style. "Ready for invasion."

"That's bad," Commander Harr said. "We don't have the men to spare now to go and fight them."

"It's dealt with," Sir Til said, in a tone that made it clear *how* it had been dealt with. "We were able to defeat them."

"The three of you?" Commander Harr asked. He looked impressed. "How many?"

"A dozen," Sir Til said.

"A dozen, and you're all whole." He looked over at Erin. "How did our newest recruit do?"

Erin swallowed, certain that this would be the moment when she found herself dismissed from the Spur, sent home, forced to go back to a life of sewing and dances rather than being the warrior she wanted to be.

"She fought well," Sir Til said. "She needs to learn to listen a little more, and to hold onto her spear better, but she killed her share, and more. She saved my life in the fight."

"Saved the life of the great Sir Til?" Commander Harr said. He looked impressed, turning to Erin. He held out his hand for her to take, clasping her wrist in his. "I'm impressed, recruit, but not surprised. I've seen how well you can fight. You'll need that, and soon."

"Because of the threat we found?" Erin asked.

Commander Harr shook his head. His expression turned serious. "It's more grave than that. We've had news from Royalsport. I have the men readying to march."

Erin frowned at that. What had happened back home? She caught herself, stopping short at the thought of the palace as home. She waited, too many thoughts running through her mind of all the things that might have gone wrong there. Was her father all right? Was her mother?

"It's Princess Lenore," Commander Harr said. "She has been captured by King Ravin's forces and taken south."

Shock flooded through Erin at that. Of all her family, Lenore had seemed like the one who was least likely to be in danger. Rodry might charge into a fight, or Vars might be cruel to the wrong person. Nerra spent all her time in the woods unprotected, and obviously Erin herself sought out danger, but Lenore? It made no sense.

"We have to get her back," Erin said. In that moment, the minor pain of her wound, or her tiredness from having ridden here from the village meant nothing. All that mattered was making sure that Lenore was all right.

"King Godwin has ordered our knights to join him in marching to secure a bridge for long enough to recover her," Commander Harr said. "You—"

"I'm going with you," Erin said, before he could command her to stay there, insist that she remain behind where it was safe.

Commander Harr nodded. "I had no plan to stop you. You're one of us, Erin. I was going to order you to hurry to be ready. You'll fight beside us, and together, we'll secure the kingdom."

"And get Lenore back," Erin said. That was the part that mattered to her, more than the rest of it.

The commander nodded again. "You have to remember that it will have taken time for the messengers to get here. I'm sure that Sir Twell and Sir Ursus rode as fast as they could, but by now, your sister could be deep into the Southern Kingdom."

"Then I'll go into it and get her back," Erin promised. "I'll tear out King Ravin's heart to do it, if I have to."

She had heard the stories growing up, of brave knights questing to recover fair maidens, saving princesses from dangers beyond reckoning. At the time, Erin had always thought that those were stupid stories. She hadn't understood why the princesses didn't just save themselves, kill the monsters, and go home to people cheering their name. *She* certainly never planned to go around waiting for a knight to come.

Now though, she *was* the knight, in all but name. She was the one who would be riding to the rescue.

"Come with me," Commander Harr said. He led the way to where armor and weapons were laid out, the knights moving among them as they selected what they needed. "I was going to leave this until you had finished proving yourself, but if it is to be war, I will not have it said that you were ill defended."

He took pieces from the stacks, passing them to Erin. Although it looked as though he was grabbing things at random, each piece seemed perfectly sized to fit Erin, chosen with the precision of long practice. He passed her a breastplate, greaves, bracers... an outer skin of plate that fit over Erin's chainmail like a glove, each piece shining and silvered.

The end result wasn't quite the full plate armor the commander wore, but instead something more mobile, with patches of chain in between the plates designed to ward off the worst of blows. He passed Erin a buckler, which she slid onto her left forearm, the shield small enough that she could still manipulate her short spear easily. Last came a half-helm to protect her head, the design of a dragon chased atop it in gold. It was the most beautiful thing Erin had seen.

"How... how is all of this here to fit me?" she asked.

Commander Harr shrugged. "You think a commander wouldn't seek out suitable protection for his troops?"

Erin didn't know what to say. "Thank you. It's... perfect."

"If you want to thank me, stay safe in the battles to come. Now, young recruit, you need to tend to your horse. We've a lot of riding to do to reach the south."

Erin nodded, running for her horse. She wouldn't let the commander down. More than that, she wouldn't let her sister down. She would help to save Lenore and beat back the Southern Kingdom's attack, whatever it took, even if it cost her life.

Chapter Twelve

The worst thing about being in chains in Lord Carrick's dungeon ... well, it was hard for Renard to pin it down to just one, really, although he'd had plenty of time to choose since they'd caught him trying to steal the gold Lord Carrick had taken from a wrecked ship bound for King Ravin. There was the strange abandonment of it, which meant that Renard probably looked even wilder than usual, red hair flying everywhere, beard crusted with mud and worse.

There were the occasional beatings, which had added a patina of bruises to his face, probably rendering his rugged good looks more rugged, but on average less ... good.

"Yselle will not be happy with you!" he called out into the dark. "None of the women will be!"

Not that it made any difference. There was no answer.

The dark and the silence were definitely on the list. If he'd had his lute, Renard would have broken the silence with song, but he hadn't, and in any case, his wrists were chained, chafing and restricting his movement. That was on the list of worst things as well. Then there was the part where he'd been sober for longer at a stretch than ever before in his life, the occasional presence of rats, the cold ...

Oh, and the part where Lord Carrick would probably have him executed at some point. As worst parts went, that one had a certain ... finality to it, although given the slow ways a man could be executed, there was no guarantee that a man couldn't find worse things still before the end.

Oh well. It had to happen sometime.

That was the problem with Renard's chosen profession: very few thieves got to retire comfortably at the end of it all. Those who didn't end up swinging on nooses tended to be killed by whatever protections rich folk had set around their goods. It was almost, almost enough to make Renard wonder why he'd chosen to be a thief at all.

Idly, he started to go back over the choices that had led to this, but the trouble was that so few of them had really counted as choices at all. They'd just been ... things he'd done, things that had seemed obvious at the time, or that he hadn't been able to keep from doing because his fingers had been too itchy *not* to take a purse, or pick a lock, or climb a wall. Trying to make any of that sound like he'd actually made a *decision* about it would be far too much.

Even when it had come to trying to steal from Lord Carrick, it hadn't been so much a decision as simply a need. Now, it seemed that he was going to die for it. At some point, when Renard had languished in his dungeon long enough, his lordship would take Renard out, try him, and decide on a suitably horrible way to kill him. All because Renard hadn't been able to walk away from the thought of coin for the taking.

Renard checked his chains for what had to be the hundredth time, just in case they had developed a flaw that he could use. Annoyingly, they were still perfect, and even if he got them off, there was still a thick door, a dungeon full of guards, and the castle's walls between him and freedom. How was a man meant to go about escaping in circumstances like that?

Renard was just settling into a nice solid round of despair when he heard the click of the lock. He braced himself, imagining that the guards had probably decided to give him another beating, but he still flinched when light streamed into the cell, harsh enough to make his eyes water after the darkness. It meant that the three figures who walked in were blurry at first.

Renard quickly found himself wishing that they had stayed that way. Instead, he was staring at three figures in dark, hooded robes, faces covered by elaborate masks that seemed to be the only individual things about their wearers. One wore a mask of interlocking greenery, another a mask with features so twisted that they seemed to hurt his eyes just looking at it. The third wore a blank white mask that gave no hint of emotion.

That was the one who spoke.

"Do you know who we are, Renard the thief?"

"Well, the masks and the robes are kind of a clue," Renard said, keeping his tone light. This was a trick, it had to be.

"And now you think that this is false," the man said. "Tell me, would even Lord Carrick impersonate *us*?"

Now Renard froze. He forced a smile even though inside, his heart was racing. It was true, no one would pretend to be this. These were the Hidden. It was said that they sought power in places most other men and women dared not even think about; that the earliest of them had been thrown out of the House of Scholars for research that should never have been attempted.

"You're trying to hide your fear," the one with the green mask said. By the voice, this one was a woman. "You think, if you're flippant enough, the bad things of the world will skate by you."

"Well, it's worked out all right so far," Renard said, jangling his chains for emphasis.

"It has left you waiting to die," the one in the twisted mask said, his voice harsh, even guttural. His mask turned toward the one who wore the blank one. "Why seek a thief who has been *caught*?"

The blank faced one did not reply, but turned back to Renard. "Would you like to be free?"

Free. The word caught Renard's attention, mostly because of the alternatives.

"And you could set me free?" he asked.

"We are here, aren't we?" the blank-faced one said. "We walked in, and we could walk out again, with you. For a price."

Of course there would be a price. People like this didn't do anything for free. From what Renard had heard, they had all paid their own prices, to things beyond the twisting and turning of reality. What would they demand? Renard decided that another question was safer.

"What do you need stolen?"

They stared at him. At least, Renard assumed that they did. With the masks, it was hard to tell.

"You've walked into a castle owned by a powerful lord with a reputation for cruelty," Renard said. "You're offering to let me go. Now, either you *really* appreciate my lute playing, or..."

"Or we need a master thief," the leader said, his blank mask providing no hint of his emotions. "Yes, we do."

"All right," Renard said. "Let's start with this: do you three have names?"

The one in the blank mask hesitated, but then seemed to relent. "I am known as Void, and these are Verdant and Wrath. Our former names were given away. Such things have power."

Renard was sure that they had all the power they could ever need. He'd heard about the Hidden.

"If you can walk in here," Renard said, "why do you need me?"

Void stood there, looking from one to the other of his companions, as if trying to decide how much to say.

"To walk into a place of men is easy," he said. "But the object we require for our ... research is in a more difficult location."

"What object, and where?" Renard asked. He said it reflexively, the way he might have with anyone who wanted him to steal for them. The fact that he was still in chains made no difference to that.

"Does it matter to you?" the one in the twisted flesh mask demanded.

But Void shrugged. "There is an amulet, locked away in a mausoleum above a volcano, protected in ways that suit your ... skills. That amulet is said to give those who wear it power over dragons."

"Dragons!" Renard said with a laugh, because who had seen dragons in years? "You must be joking. Is that what this is? Lord Carrick's idea of a ..."

He didn't finish, because the woman in the mask of greenery leaned close to him. Verdant's eyes ... they seemed to start green, but then shifted to red, glowing from within with a fire that stole the breath out of him. Somehow, Renard suspected that this was one woman he wouldn't be able to charm with a few well-chosen songs and compliments.

"We do not joke," she said, as she moved back. "And we do not like having our time wasted."

"Your time too," Void said. "How long now until Lord Carrick drags you from here to your death?"

He had a point. Even so ...

"No, thank you," he said.

"What?" Wrath demanded, and he looked as though he might strike out at Renard in that moment.

"You think I haven't heard rumors of the Hidden?" Renard asked. "I've sung enough songs in my time to hear those too."

"They have written beautiful songs about us," Verdant said. "But few true ones."

Renard suspected that there was enough truth hidden away in those songs though; that the Hidden were collectors of power, to whom good and evil were irrelevant; that they could do things to a man that would imperil his very soul. Compared to all of that, even Lord Carrick didn't seem so bad.

"There are things we could do to you if you refuse," Void said.

"And then you still wouldn't have a thief," Renard pointed out.

"You would really refuse freedom? You would really choose death?"

Renard nodded. "If the alternative is going with you, yes."

It turned out that he'd found a new worst thing. Compared to this one, even all the others didn't seem so bad.

Void gestured to the others. "Very well. Come. We must do this… another way."

He turned, walking out of the cell, the robed forms of the others following in his wake. The door shut behind him with a bang, the lock clicking back into place. Renard supposed it was too much to ask that they might leave it open.

Even as he settled back to wait for his death again, he couldn't help feeling that he'd just avoided something far, far worse.

Chapter Thirteen

Rodry and his friends raced into the landscape of the south, trying to catch up to his sister, while Rodry hoped against hope that he would be in time. They rode down paved trackways and over dirt roads, following the signs of the party that had been ahead of them ever since they crossed into this country.

For what had to be the hundredth time since the river crossing, Rodry cursed his brother Vars. Had he been a little braver, they might have had Lenore back by now, and the ones who had taken her might already be dead. When Rodry returned, their father would hear every detail of his cowardice.

For now, there was only the chase after Lenore.

One thing that surprised Rodry a little was how much the landscape had changed simply by crossing the river, as if the whole climate differed just with that small shift. There were trees here, but they were olive and fig as often as apple, the forests light and hot rather than the rain-filled landscapes of the Northern Kingdom. The ground around seemed drier, and Rodry was sure that they had ridden past at least a couple of vineyards, set into the sides of hills. The people they had seen dressed as simply as peasant folk back home, but differently as well, with slashed skirts and blouses in place of dresses, broad hats in place of hoods. It seemed that almost everyone wore a flash of red or purple somewhere too, perhaps in homage to King Ravin.

They shrank back away from Rodry and the others as they passed, perhaps sensing some of the fury of their mission.

"How much further to this hunting lodge?" Rodry asked Kay.

His friend shook his head. "I don't know, Rodry. I only know that it even exists because of my father."

"What use is knowing that a place exists if you don't know where it is?" Rodry demanded, and then bit back his anger. He wasn't his brother, to lash out at those who didn't deserve it. "We ride on."

And in riding, they had to hope that they were going in the right direction. Seris, Mautlice, and the others were doing their best to track the group ahead, the way they might have done when hunting, and a whole traveling party was easier to track than any deer might have been, but even so, what if they took a wrong turn? What if they rode right into the heart of Ravin's kingdom, but couldn't find the place in it where they were keeping Lenore?

The answer to that was simple: they would burn Ravin's kingdom until they found her.

They paused in a spot where the trail branched a dozen different ways, tall, arching trees rising up around in a rough circle. There was a low hut there, barely more than a lean-to, while around, the ground was churned up as if it had seen far more than a dozen riders come through there. There were bushes and rocks around the diverging paths, some set here and there with candles, as if the whole place were some great shrine or meeting place. Rodry saw it as far more than that though.

He saw it as the perfect place for an ambush.

"Down!" he yelled, as arrows flew from the bushes, throwing himself from his horse even as a shaft flashed past where his head had been. Around him, he saw his soldiers and friends duck, or raise their shields, or fling themselves from their horses the way Rodry had. Some weren't quick enough. He saw Mautlice spin, blank-faced, from the saddle, a crossbow bolt sticking from his chest. A soldier took an arrow in the shoulder, crying out in pain.

The enemy poured out of their hiding places then, and it seemed that half a dozen of them were dressed in odd clothes, carrying a strange selection of weapons that marked them out as Quiet Men rather than normal soldiers. There were those too, though, red tunics marking them as King Ravin's troops, armed with spears and short bows.

"You didn't think that we'd notice you following, Prince Rodry?" one of the Quiet Men said, drawing a pair of long knives. He was tall and shaven headed, the glint of oiled chainmail showing here and there under his clothes. "You didn't think we'd be waiting?"

Rodry drew his longsword as he stood, taking it in two hands, holding back his anger just for a second.

"You're one of the ones who took my sister?" he demanded.

The Quiet Man nodded. "Shall I tell you everything that we did to her while we had her to ourselves? Shall I detail every last—"

Rodry struck out in the middle of the man's words, his anger driving him forward into the attack. The Quiet Man caught that attack on his knives, but Rodry was already twisting away, cutting down toward his foe's legs. He heard the crunch of bone as the blade struck home, but he had to fall back to avoid the next sweep of the man's knives.

Rodry's friends charged forward then, taking their cue from him, while the soldiers jumped in to support them. He heard the sudden clash of blades, and the screams of the dying. In that moment, everything was chaos, the ambush unfolding around him in one continuous stream.

One of King Ravin's soldiers appeared in front of him, and Rodry hacked him down with an overhead stroke. He felt a blade bounce from his armor, turned, and kicked another soldier away.

One of the Quiet Men, a woman, had a strangling rope around Kay's neck, pulling tight and hanging on close as a lover. Rodry lunged forward, plunging his longsword up under her ribs, no hint of remorse at cutting down one of those who had hurt his sister, only satisfaction. Kay turned and nodded his thanks, then barely parried a sword blow in time.

Rodry had no time to help with this foe, because the one with the two knives was there again before him, staggering forward on one leg, cutting high and low. Rodry gave ground, looking for room to wield his longsword in full strokes, but the Quiet Man kept pressing forward, giving him no room to strike the way he wanted to. Rodry had to twist and turn, using the bracers of his armor to deflect thrust after thrust.

Rodry heard the scrape of someone behind him, felt the whisper of something heading toward his head. If he hadn't spent so long training in the House of Weapons, he might have done the foolish thing and turned to face the new threat. Instead, Rodry dropped to his knees, thrusting up over his shoulder with his longsword. He heard a cry as a curved sword passed over his head, felt the give of flesh under the thrust of his sword's point. He ripped it out, then struck forward with the pommel of his sword, catching his attacker in the stomach and doubling him over.

Rodry came back up to his feet, half turning as he brought his longsword around in a great swing that hacked through his opponent's neck and kept going into the dirt. It stuck there for a moment, and the foe he'd struck at over his shoulder all but fell into him. They went down together, neither of them holding their sword anymore, both of them punching and kneeing and grabbing while around them the fight continued to rage. An elbow smashed into Rodry's face, a knee struck his stomach. He clung on for dear life, because he could feel his opponent weakening, the blood pouring from him thanks to the wound Rodry had inflicted.

Then Rodry saw his foe starting to reach down for a knife at his belt and knew that if he reached it, it wouldn't matter how much greater Rodry's strength or stamina was, because he would slide that blade into a gap in Rodry's armor as easy as breathing.

Rodry grabbed for his foe's arm in desperation, forcing it away from the weapon. They rolled, and Rodry came up on top, striking down with an armored forearm again and again. He heard the crunch of bone, but kept going, until it seemed that blood filled the whole world, and the foe beneath him went limp. Only then did Rodry dare stand, snatching up his longsword, looking around for another foe to fight.

There were none; his friends and the soldiers with them stood victorious, or most of them did. Mautlice still lay unmoving on the ground, and two of the soldiers who had accompanied them lay just as dead. Rodry wondered what he would be able to say to Mautlice's father, and he simply didn't know.

It was worse for King Ravin's forces. Around them, King Ravin's men lay dead or dying.

"Take their tunics and their flags," Rodry ordered his men. "We might need them, soon enough."

Only one of King Ravin's forces still stood. One of the Quiet Men stood with his back to a tree, sword out, surrounded by Rodry's men. Rodry stormed over, pointing to him.

"Where is she?" he demanded. "Which way?"

"I surrender to you," the Quiet Man said. He dropped his sword. "It is said that you are a brave and noble prince, so you will not cut a man down in cold blood."

"Which *way*?" Rodry demanded again.

The Quiet Man said nothing, but his glance to one of the paths was enough. They would find the tracks, would find where Lenore had been taken.

As for this one, who had been part of this, who had done unspeakable things to his sister… Rodry stepped forward then, sword back behind his shoulders.

"You would not," the Quiet Man said. "You would not murder a prisoner."

He took one large step level with the tree, letting out a cry of pure rage as he struck in a horizontal blow. The Quiet Man looked at Rodry in shock as the weapon struck home, slicing through flesh to cut deep into the bark of the tree behind him. He tumbled, headless, eyes still staring.

"This is not murder," Rodry said, spitting into the dirt. "It's an execution."

Chapter Fourteen

From the moment Odd arrived on the shores of the kingdom, his small boat bumping against a rocky shore, he knew that he needed to head south, to Royalsport. He needed to warn the king of the impending invasion via Leveros, needed to save the kingdom from what was to come.

Maybe that would even make up for some of the things he had done in his life.

No, nothing would do that. Penitence as a monk he had not, even though he still wore their robes, still had the shaved head of their order. No amount of prayer or meditation had brought him peace, and when the attack on the island had come…the man he had been was there waiting inside him.

He shook his head and started walking, up off the shoreline, scrambling up a slope of sandy rocks until he reached the top of a cliff. There were trees in the distance, thick and green and tangled, with only the faintest of paths leading into them. From the position of the sun, it seemed that they were to the south. The right way then.

The small wounds he'd suffered on the island ached now, but he kept walking, because if there was one thing the monastery had taught him, it was patient endurance. With every step, he could feel the movement of his sheathed sword at his back, long and slender, enclosed in a covering of black leather for now. It was an unfamiliar feeling after so long in the monastery, but at the same time the most familiar feeling of all. There had been a time when he hadn't felt alive without a sword in his hand, the thrill of battle running through his veins.

The abbot would not approve of that, if he was still alive. Odd suspected that he was not, when his whole plan had been to offer himself up to the soldiers as a kind of sacrifice. He suspected that *any* monk who had remained on the Isle of Leveros would be slaughtered now; King Ravin's men were almost as bloodthirsty as...

...as he had been.

Images came to him, of villages sacked, people slaughtered. Many had been the armored forms of worthy foes, bandits and rebels, but many more had not been. The faces of women and children mingled with those of others he had killed, and the worst part was that Odd couldn't even make out specific ones. He hadn't been watching closely enough for that when he'd been Sir Oderick the Mad, consumed by battle rage, consumed by the love of the fight.

"I am not him," Odd told himself aloud, as if the certainty of that would make the words true. There had been a reason why he hadn't brought his noble's clothes, or his armor.

Yet who was he? Not a monk, not a knight, not...anything. At best, a messenger, whose sole purpose was to warn the kingdom of what was coming on the flank they didn't know about. That *was* a purpose, though, and Odd would fulfill it, whatever it took.

He kept walking.

How long he kept walking, Odd didn't know. At one point, he came to a crofter's hut, pieced together from aged planks and turf squares for a roof. The crofter's wife came to the door, offering him a bowl of soup, clearly seized from an already bubbling bowl.

"You could stay for the night," she said. "A monk in the house is said to be lucky."

"I am anything but lucky," Odd assured her, and pressed a coin into her hand before he kept walking. Somewhere in his walking, day might have turned to night and back again, but it was hard to tell under the canopy of the trees. He lit a candle and kept going, until tiredness forced him to stop.

In the morning, he knelt in meditation, the way he had for so many mornings now. His mind would not still itself though, and if he had prayers within him, he could not bring himself to say them. Odd rose instead and continued on his trek. In the midmorning, he came upon another hut of forest folk, and along with a little bread and cheese, these sold him a mule they had grazing behind the house.

Compared to all the mounts he'd had in his time, it was easily the humblest. Sir Oderick the Mad had ridden stallions and war-trained chargers, not dappled mules that seemed to snort with every step as if in contempt of the world. His saddles had been finely wrought, not blankets laid simply across a beast's back. Still, it meant that he could move south quicker, and that was all that mattered.

He sat upon his mule and tried to use the jolting of it as a different kind of meditation, but somehow the beast managed to move without even a consistent rhythm, jarring Odd from his thoughts every few steps as it seemed that the mule found bones in its back Odd had not suspected a steed could have. He knew he must look ludicrous like this, a far cry from the noble he had been, and Odd laughed at the foolishness of it all, long and loud.

"What's so funny, priest?" The first man to step from the forest was a bear of a man, huge and broad shouldered, dark-bearded and dressed in rough clothes suitable for a day of felling trees. Scraps of leathers serving as armor said that his days held more violence than that though, and the axe he held was a thing of war, not just work.

The second man was smaller, hard faced and armed with a long, single-edged knife, a nail hammered into the hilt to serve as a cross guard. Together, they looked like the kind of men who were farmers or foresters some days, bandits others, drifting back and forth across the line to lawlessness. Odd had seen many men like them before.

"I'm not a priest," Odd said, stepping down from his mule. "I *was* a monk, but my abbot told me that I was no longer welcome. As for what's funny, I suppose that's just how far I've fallen."

"Things can always get worse," the big one said, fingering his axe.

"True," Odd said. He didn't reach for his sword, not yet.

"How about you give us what you have, and they won't?" the smaller one said.

Odd laughed again, and if these men had known him, they would have known the strange, mad edge in that laugh. "Really, boys, is that the best you can do? I mean, yes, good, menacing approach, but if you're robbing someone, you should make more of an effort."

"How about I make the effort to split your head open?" the axe man suggested.

Odd's laugh wouldn't stop now, not even when the big one swung the axe at his head. He was still laughing when he sidestepped, still laughing when he kicked the thug in the knee, sending him sprawling. He didn't draw his sword yet, but took it from his back, sheath and all, using it like a club to smash the long knife from the other one's hands. Odd spun and kicked him square in the stomach, sending him to the ground alongside his friend.

Idly, Odd noticed that his mule was at the side of the path, chewing grass as if nothing were happening. The madness in him found that as funny as all the rest of it, so that he laughed even while he drew his sword.

There was no blood on it yet, but his mind's eye supplied all the ways that blood could run through the etchings on the steel, all the ways that redness could fill in the dips and furrows of it, picking out the knots and the whorls on the surface. He stood there, holding back the urge to kill only with difficulty, smiling at the two would-be robbers like the demented thing he was.

"Best run, boys," he said. "I'm a little out of practice, but two on one is hardly even worth the effort."

"What about eight?" another voice said behind him.

Half a dozen other men stepped from the trees, and a part of Odd cursed himself for not seeing that coming. They were dressed in similar ways to the others, in scraps of leathers, mostly armed with hatchets or knives. They had obviously hung back just in case Odd had friends hidden out of sight, in case this was a trap laid to catch those who might rob travelers.

Odd smiled at them. "I take it that you still want my money pouch?"

"And your sword, and your mule," the large one said.

"Ah now," Odd replied. "I have become quite attached to that mule. Besides, I need it to head south."

"You'll give us all of it, or we'll gut you," the short one with the knife said.

Of course, the sensible, even sane thing to do would be to give them all that they wanted. It was what the abbot would have done, no doubt. Even most warriors had the sense to know when they were outnumbered too badly. To charge in would be madness.

"But then," Odd said aloud, ignoring the men's looks of confusion, "I am, famously, mad."

"What are you–" the one with the beard began, but by that point, Odd was already charging, sword held high.

Chapter Fifteen

Erin rode back and forth along the column of knights heading south, frustrated that she could, frustrated that they weren't charging along at a full gallop. Around her, the Knights of the Spur shone atop their horses, their armor and barding glinting in the sun, but that only seemed to make it worse; it made it seem like a parade, rather than a charge to save her sister.

They were crossing the farmland south of the Spur, the column of knights shining against the green and gold of the fields, but they weren't far off the forests that covered so much of the ground between them and Royalsport now. It still didn't seem like they'd gone far enough; not even close.

Erin reached the front, where Commander Harr sat atop a horse so large it barely seemed like a horse at all beneath its armor, more like some steel-clad monster. A pennant flew from his lance, with the image of the spur outlined against a blue background.

"You seem to be riding three leagues for every one the rest of us manage," Commander Harr said, his tone far too calm for Erin's taste, given that they were riding to war. Shouldn't he have sounded more urgent, more worried for Lenore's safety?

"We're going too slowly!" Erin said. "We could be riding twice as fast as this."

"For a day, perhaps," Commander Harr said. "But then we would have to stop. Even if we did make it to the river in a hurry, we would be exhausted when it came to any fighting."

"But we're the Knights of the Spur!" Erin insisted. "Aren't you supposed to be warriors out of legend, able to fight all day, against any enemy?"

"And because of that, the king expects us to be *able* to fight his enemies when we arrive," Commander Harr said. "Resume your place in the ranks. There is much marching still to go."

"I know how far there is to go," Erin said. "That's the problem."

Commander Harr raised one closed fist, and behind him, the entire column drew to a halt, stopping with the kind of discipline that only the Knights of the Spur could manage.

"I gave you an order, recruit," he said.

"You think that's the most important thing right now?" Erin shot back. "When my sister's out there somewhere, in the hands of King Ravin, you think *that's* the thing that matters?"

"I think it matters whether I can trust you to do what you're commanded, no matter what you're feeling," Commander Harr said. "I think the lives of your companions might depend on how well you can do that."

"I won't endanger the others," Erin said, but even as she said it, she itched to keep riding. Every second they wasted here was another in which her sister was growing further away.

"Won't you?" Commander Harr demanded. "Til, Fenir, get up here!"

The two knights rode forward, coming to a halt before Erin and the commander.

"You said that Erin here was a little too eager," Commander Harr said. "What does that mean? What did she do at the village?"

To Erin's surprise, the two knights hesitated a moment, obviously caught between loyalty to their leader and to her.

"The truth!" Commander Harr bellowed.

"She charged into the village," Til said. "I told her to hold off, but she went in anyway."

"Fought well though," Fenir said.

"It doesn't matter how she fought!" Commander Harr said. "Not if we can't trust her to hold back when she needs to." He turned to Erin. "Even now, I can see you twitching, like you want to ride for the horizon to save your sister."

"Lenore's in danger," Erin shot back. How could he expect her to stand there when they were wasting *time*?

"And if she's in danger when we reach the bridges, you'll abandon your companions and do what you feel you must to save her?" Commander Harr asked.

Erin didn't even understand why it was a question.

"No," Commander Harr said. "I can see that I made a mistake, bringing you. You will return to the fortress, for your own safety, and for ours."

"You...you can't ask me to do that!" Erin said, unable to believe that Commander Harr would even contemplate it.

"I am not *asking*," the commander said. "Remember that you are under my command."

Erin bit back her counterargument, knowing that there was no way that she would be able to convince the commander, not in time. Instead, she offered a bow, leaning low over the back of her horse.

"Very well..." she said, then heeled her horse into a run.

Commander Harr bellowed behind her for her to stop, but Erin didn't even slow. She glanced back, half expecting to see knights charging after her, but they were stock-still in their positions, obeying their leader's command to halt in a way that she never could. Commander Harr called something else then, and Fenir and Til set off after her, but Erin was already well ahead, already galloping clear of them.

She galloped for the forest, knowing that in the shelter of the trees they wouldn't find her. She plunged under the shelter of the branches, following the path, not slowing down. Her horse leapt over a fallen log, its hooves thundering against the dirt of the track. Erin ducked under a branch, kept her head low, kept riding.

The sounds of pursuit faded behind her, but Erin kept going. She didn't want to risk being dragged back to the fort when she could help her sister. She had to keep going, couldn't slow down now.

So she rode, and kept riding, until her horse slowed of its own volition, unwilling to gallop any further. Erin walked it then, leaping down from the saddle because she didn't want to risk pushing it to exhaustion. She walked along the forest track, certain now that the knights would be long behind her, probably still moving at a snail's pace. She would reach the bridges before them, would find her sister...

A sound drew Erin from those thoughts, though: the sound of steel on steel, coming together in violence. Erin looked around, not certain where it was coming from in the close confines of the forest, but quickly realized that it lay ahead, along the track.

Perhaps Commander Harr would have counseled caution, ordered her to hold back. Erin couldn't do so, though, not when someone might be in danger. Tying her horse's reins to a tree, she took her spear and hurried forward, ready to help.

⚜ ⚜ ⚜

The only advantage to fighting eight men at once, as Odd saw it, was that at least anyone he struck out at was likely to be an enemy. He slashed and cut, keeping his foes at bay with the sheer fury of his sword work, so that coming forward at him would have been like wandering into a hailstorm made of steel.

Even so, some of the bandits tried it. The one with the beard hacked at him with that axe of his, and Odd wove away from it, catching the head on his cross guard and knocking the man back. He parried another blow from a knife, ducked in behind a tree, and popped out of the other side in time to thrust his point in between a man's ribs. The bandit gasped and stumbled, but still aimed a clumsy blow at Odd's head.

Odd was already moving, the battle madness flowing through him now as he laughed in his fury. The world seemed such a strange place in moments like these, joyous and terrifying and anger filled all at once, the sharp edges of no more moment than the trees around him. One scraped at Odd's arm, and he must have *felt* the pain, but his main concern was hacking back with a diagonal stroke that all but cut the other man in two.

He danced between the trees, and between the blades, knowing that to stay still against so many men was to die. Not that Odd usually cared about dying, but to do so before he had delivered his message would be ... unfortunate. He saw the big man with the axe again, ran forward for him, but the smaller knifeman was there instead. Odd saw that long knife flashing for his skull and swayed back, cutting up from underneath to slam his blade into his foe's hands, taking them off at the wrist while he screamed.

That was two, maybe three if the one he'd stabbed died soon. Given that there were still six left, that was a bad thing. One against six was not a situation a man could survive, especially unarmored. That was why Odd gave ground, dodging between the trees, forcing them to come at him singly, where he could fight them.

It wasn't like he was going to *run.*

He grinned as another came at him, ducked under the sweep of a blade, drove his shoulder into the man's gut. As he fell back, Odd aimed a swipe at his throat, but there was a branch in the way. Besides, there was another man coming in from the side: the big one. Odd had been wondering where he'd gone. He parried another blow of the axe, but the big man slammed into him, knocking him sprawling.

He *should* have died then, because hitting and moving against so many was one thing, but knocked to the ground against them was dead, no matter how audacious you were. The big man loomed over Odd, axe raised, and it seemed to Odd that he should have been truly terrified in that moment, should have *cared* that his life was about to come to an end in the middle of a forest for no real reason.

He'd never been much good at meditating back at the monastery, but there was a kind of meditation in this, in watching the rise of the axe, sinking into the flow of the battle, seeing the trees overhead, seeing the head of a spear sprouting from the axe man's chest...

Wait, that wasn't right, was it?

A figure stepped from behind his opponent as the axe man fell, the light shining behind them so that it took Odd a moment to realize that this was a girl who couldn't be more than fifteen or sixteen. She wore nearly full armor, plate over chain, in the fashion of the Knights of the Spur, and there was something set, almost hard, about her features. In that moment, she was already turning, parrying the blow of a long knife with her buckler, bringing her spear around to slash at another man.

Odd was on his feet then, rushing to her side, cutting left and right at the foes who came at him. One tried an overhead stroke and Odd didn't even parry, just rushed inside it as he cut across the man's stomach to bring him down. He beat aside another blow from the side, and saw the girl lance her spear into another man's heart. Odd bounded close to one of the bandits, turned his wrists, hacked through his throat. He spun ...

The forest was empty now except for him and the girl, who stood over the last of their foes, her spear wet with blood. Odd stood there, sword raised, forcing himself to breathe slowly, to work past the battle madness that insisted he should keep fighting just for the sheer joy of it. It seemed to take forever before he could lower his blade, clean it, sheathe it.

"I'm Odd," he said, because none of the other names he had fit him anymore.

"I ..." The girl frowned. "That's a name?"

Odd nodded. "Might be someone's idea of a description too, I suppose. This is usually the part where you tell me your name, knight."

"What makes you think I'm a knight?" she asked.

Odd raised an eyebrow. "Well, the armor is a clue. Also, I've ... seen them fight." He didn't want to tell her all of it, or they really *would* be fighting. "You're a Knight of the Spur, aren't you?"

"I ..." She hesitated before she nodded, suggesting that things were more complicated, but Odd was used to complicated. "My name's Erin."

"Lady Erin," Odd said. He assumed that even the Knights of the Spur wouldn't just call a girl knight *sir.* "Just that, or have they given you a nickname yet?"

"Not yet," she said. "And it's ... just Erin."

"Give them time," he assured her. They'd been the first ones to call him the Mad, after all. "What brings you out into the forest, just Erin? Aside from saving the likes of me?"

Maybe that *was* the point, though. They said that the world was kind to fools and madmen. Maybe this kind of savior was what kindness looked like.

"I'm traveling to save my sister," the girl said.

"Save her from what?" Odd asked.

"King Ravin's forces have taken her south, over the Slate. They say he plans to invade."

Odd froze at those words. Could it be a coincidence that here, in the middle of nowhere, he would run into a knight who knew about the threat from King Ravin? Surely it had to be fate, or a sign? The abbot had always said that the world fit together in more complex ways than a human mind could hold. Maybe this was one.

"What are *you* doing out here?" Erin asked. "There can't be many monks wandering the forest. Still fewer monks carrying swords."

Odd thought about explaining who he was, but that would cause too many problems. Instead, he gestured to the way he'd come.

"I came here from Leveros to warn of a threat from King Ravin," Odd said. "His men have taken the island, and I fear they plan to use it as a staging point to invade without crossing the bridges. I seek those with the power to help: the knights, or the king."

"I could... help get your message to both," Erin said.

"And I could help you to recover your sister," Odd replied. It seemed strange to be promising this, when he already had a task, but there had to be a reason that he had met this girl here, like this.

She looked around, and Odd knew that she was looking over the bodies, seeing the violence he had done. Ordinarily, people looked at him with horror when they saw that, but now, Odd saw hope. This was one case when a man of violence was more use than one of prayer.

"You swear you'll help me find her?" Erin asked.

Odd nodded. "On my oath as a..." What was he now? What had he ever been? "On my oath."

"And I swear I'll help you spread the word about the invasion," Erin said.

Odd took her hand. Her grip was strangely strong for her size, but then, she *was* a knight. It had been a long time since Odd had ridden beside one, let alone on a mission to save a lost young woman. For a moment, just a moment, he felt like a hero.

Still, he was sure that the feeling would pass once the killing began.

Chapter Sixteen

In the circle of light within the vaulted chamber, Devin worked at the forge until his arms ached with it, trying to get the star metal to respond as it should, trying to get the magic to do all that he wanted.

It was harder than he could have believed, but the most frustrating part of it all was that sometimes it *did* work. Sometimes, magic rippled out, so that only Master Grey's runes, set into every surface, contained it. On those times, the metal responded to him, shifting in response to his touch, but that only served to make all the other times that much more frustrating.

How much time had he spent down here working now? How many attempts had he made? Too many attempts to truly count now, and the frustration of that was only made greater because he was not one of the men who had gone south toward the bridge, trying to get Princess Lenore back.

He *wanted* to be, wanted to be the one who could save her, clasp her hand in his, bring her back to safety. He wanted to know that she was well, and happy, but more than that, he wanted to be the one to do it, wanted her to look at him as a savior. It was the closest that a peasant like him would ever get to... no, he couldn't think like that, had to focus on this.

Master Grey had told him as much; had told him that this was the crucial part he had to play. Yet Devin couldn't see *how* it was crucial that he stayed here and learned to use the flickers of magic that had come to him before, how it was important that he was able to forge a sword, or that he had strange dreams.

Master Grey certainly wasn't here to explain any of it. The sorcerer had gone, off about some task that he hadn't even begun to explain.

If he'd gone, though, there might be an opportunity in that. It meant that his rooms would be empty. It meant that there might actually be a chance to find out more about all of the things that the sorcerer wouldn't talk about, to find out about his birth, and why he had been given to strangers to raise ...

Making a decision, Devin set down his hammer.

He walked up the steps from the basement forge, the light from torches marking out a stone-walled path for him to follow. He followed it up, the blankness of the walls finally giving way to tapestries and statues, nooks and carved posts as he came out into the body of the castle.

It seemed quiet compared to what Devin knew, but only because the times that he'd seen it before, it had been in the grip of either a wedding feast or preparations for a rescue. Now, there were servants, and a few nobles here and there, but not the crowds of guests that there had been before. He stopped one of the servants, who looked at him nervously, clearly not knowing who he was.

"Which way do I go to Master Grey's tower from here?" he asked.

That made the servant's eyes widen in obvious fear, and they pointed in silence. It seemed like the best that Devin was going to get. He set off in the direction they pointed, down a hall where red floor tiles were cracked with age, and the walls held pictures over which drapes had been drawn, as if to shield them from view. More secrets; why was everything close to Master Grey a secret?

Devin eventually found a stone arch, with a light wooden door set into it. The door had a star carved upon it, the center a kind of face that looked out, eyes smooth and blank, as if blind. There was no lock on the door, but as Devin pushed at it, it didn't give. He tried again, setting his hand on that star shape to push ...

Some flicker of power rose up inside him, and Devin felt the door give way. Within, there were stairs, these ones made of marble edged with pale ash, circling around an open center to the tower, so that it seemed all too possible for Devin to plunge to his death if he put a foot wrong. Looking down as he rose, he could see lines strung across from one point on the stairs to another, forming a kind of net. Except that it wasn't a net, because

Devin had seen the mystical symbols Master Grey had used in the forge. This was one of those, only much larger.

He kept climbing until he reached the top of the tower. There, the stairs gave way to a broad room, with another set of stairs leading up from it. This room was filled with accoutrements that seemed to point to Master Grey's profession: brass instruments and glass vials set on tables, books arranged on shelves, held in place by goblets or alchemist's tools, or, in one case, a skull set with jewels.

A table stood to one side, covered in charts and papers as if Master Grey had been trying to work something out. There were maps, of the Northern Kingdom, the Southern Kingdom, and another landmass that could only be Sarrass. There were marks on some of the maps: intersecting lines that seemed to indicate an attempt to narrow something down. A pendulum with a golden chain sat atop one of the maps.

All of it suggested that Master Grey was working on something Devin didn't understand, but that was hardly a revelation. He needed information instead, needed to know what was going on. Devin started to search the books on the wall, hoping that there might be some clue hidden there.

Most were indecipherable. They held diagrams that made no sense, or notes in languages Devin had never even seen, let alone knowing how to read them. There were other notes, written in a hand that had to be Master Grey's, but they talked about experiments or the qualities of substances, the value of powdered pearl set against a bezoar, the usefulness of gold in outlining runes...

Devin headed up the next set of stairs, finding a room that was almost bare in comparison to the one below. There was a bed in there, carved from slats of wood that seemed so old they were almost fossilized. The rest of it was blank, with white daubed walls that would have been plain, except that someone had inscribed mark after mark in red, purple, and gold.

There was a trunk there, again with no lock, as with the door. Just as with the door though, something rose up in Devin as he touched it, and the slats of the box seemed to move in response, sliding back like the petals of a flower unfolding.

There were objects within: a set of robes, a ring of gold, a ring made from polished wood, a glass globe held in a hand that seemed to have been carved from stone. There was a book, too, bound in leather that had been stained with what looked like blood, but also with something a deep, azure blue. It was so thick that Devin could barely contain it in one hand.

Devin opened the covers, and found Master Grey's writing within. There were more notes of the kind that he'd seen below, but there were also private things, personal notes on everything from the feelings of the king to the progress of a project that seemed to consume much of his thoughts. It was a diary of sorts, mixed with a notebook, and Devin found himself flicking back through it, trying to understand why the magus had gone to him, had sought him out.

Every second that he stood there, his heart pounded. Devin didn't know where Master Grey had gone, which meant he didn't know how long it might be before he returned. He was only too aware that he had no excuse if the other man appeared there, and he didn't want to think about all the things that a magus might be able to do to those who angered him.

He needed to know though. Any danger was worth the risk.

Devin kept looking back through the journal, until finally, he found a single entry that made his breath catch.

I have located a boy born on the night that the dragons flew, one who was not killed. There are signs that he may have power; signs that he might be the new magus that the kingdom, the world, needs as the dragons come and the nations fall into blood. He may change the course of all of this. The weapon will be the first test, and the rest will follow. He must be the one. Already, I can feel my days growing shorter…

Devin stared at that. He'd known that he had magic, but this ... it hit him like a punch to the gut. He didn't know what to think, the enormity of it too great, the weight of it settling on him. Master Grey made it sound as if Devin were his *replacement*, not just his student. More than that, he made it sound as if a terrible threat was coming, and Devin ... somehow he was supposed to be the one to save them.

Chapter Seventeen

The hunting lodge was like a small fortress in itself, so that Rodry found himself looking at it the way he might have a castle he was about to lay siege to. He needed to find a way in, needed to find a way to get to his sister, needed to get her out of there.

The difficult part was that all of the same elements that served to make the lodge work for hunting made it defensible too. It had rings of ditches around it, probably there to keep game in place for hunters, but they would slow horses just as easily. It had wooden towers from which to spot deer or stranger beasts and shoot them, but those would let soldiers fire down at attackers just as well. The stone walls might serve to keep guests warm, but they would keep enemies out, too.

Then there were the soldiers there. They camped at the edge of the hunting grounds, at least a small regiment of them, clearly preparing for war. There were spearmen there and archers, knights and swordsmen, all in a camp flying King Ravin's colors, surrounded by wooden stakes.

"Please tell me that there's a plan," Kay said, with obvious nervousness.

"They'll have taken Lenore to the lodge," Rodry guessed. He could see horses tied up outside it. "We ride up like we belong there. We wear King Ravin's colors so that the soldiers think it's their own returning from ambushing us, and hope that gets us inside."

"That's why you had us take the tunics and flags?" Kay guessed.

Rodry nodded. He'd planned for this. He didn't say how fragile that plan was, how easily someone might recognize them by all the ways in which their forces clearly weren't the ones that had set out to intercept his. He didn't say that, in any other circumstances, he would hold off, find a different plan, do this another way.

There was no other way; his sister was in danger.

So he pulled on the red of King Ravin's forces, set off in the direction of the lodge, and tried to pretend that all was well. He and the others were far enough from the encampment that they wouldn't be able to make out individual faces, just the red that proclaimed them to be on the same side. He saw one of the soldiers wave, and ignored it, kept riding.

There were two guardsmen by the doors to the hunting lodge, and the closer Rodry and the others got, the more concerned they looked. A hundred yards off, and they looked surprised that so many men would be coming at the lodge. Fifty, and they were shouting, trying to ready their weapons.

Rodry hit the first of them even as he stepped forward, ordering Rodry to halt. His sword swept down, all but cutting the man in half. Beside him, the sergeant lanced a spear through the chest of the second.

"Go, your highness," the man said. "We'll hold the way for you."

There was no time for hesitation now, no time for thought. Rodry leapt down from his horse, Kay, Seris and his other friends following in his wake while the soldiers from Vars's regiment spread out around the entrance to the hunting lodge, ready to hold it against any who came.

Rodry stepped up to the hunting lodge's door and kicked it with one booted foot. It was barred, but it was only wood, and not truly designed to hold back a determined attacker. On the second kick, it splintered. On the third, it gave way, letting Rodry and his friends pour into a hallway lined with wooden panels, and hung with the trophy heads of creatures killed there for King Ravin's sport. Rodry saw deer and bear, wolf and stranger things, like the skull of a beast with three horns and wicked teeth, or a bull-like creature that seemed strangely human in its expression. There were doors on every side, obviously leading to the various rooms of the lodge. A broad teak staircase headed up toward a second floor hung with the hides of creatures. There were statues there to King Ravin's greatness, while the far wall was painted with a scene of him hunting a beast that towered over him.

Rodry had no time to take in the details, though, because an enemy was already running at him, short sword in hand.

The man lunged for Rodry, and Rodry managed to turn out of the way, battering his foe against the wall hard enough to crack the wainscoting. He saw Kay finish him, but Rodry was already moving on.

"Lenore! Lenore, where are you?"

Another foe came at Rodry, and this time he felt a spear skitter from his armor. He hacked back at the man's legs, bringing him down.

"Lenore!"

"Rodry!"

A single shout came from somewhere above, cut off as if a hand had been hastily placed over Lenore's mouth. Or as if something worse had happened.

More foes came out of the doors at ground level, rushing forward in a mass as they started to recover from the shock of being attacked so suddenly. Rodry's friends met them with steel, but he pressed forward, shouldering a man aside, battering away a blow from another. He had to get to Lenore. A man stood ahead of him on the stairs and Rodry lanced the point of his sword through a gap in his foe's armor, ignoring the impact as a mace slammed into his side. He threw the enemy down into the melee below, saw the body slam into Seris's opponent to knock him back.

Rodry continued up the stairs, to a landing lined with wooden doors. He kicked one, then the next, searching for Lenore, determined to get to her. The last of them opened before he could kick it, and he stumbled forward into a bedroom where the windows were covered with barred slats. One of the Quiet Men was there waiting for him: a woman who slipped a strangling cord around his throat. Across the room, a man held Lenore, one arm around her throat, a sword in his other hand.

Rodry knew he could deal with the woman easily, because all he had to do was reverse his sword, but the moment he did that, the man would be free to strike at Lenore. Even as he thought about it, the strangling rope was tightening about his throat, cutting off his air, making it hard to even think.

He did two things simultaneously: he threw his sword, flinging it point first, and he threw himself backward, throwing himself and his attacker into the wall. He felt his full weight, along with the hardness of his armor, slam into his foe, smashing the breath out of her, loosening her grip even as it sent them both down to the floor. At the same time, he saw his sword plunge into the skull of the man there, bringing him down, sending him toppling backward.

Lenore cried out as he fell away from her, but she reacted faster than Rodry could have hoped. She grabbed for the man's weapon, snatching it up and throwing it in Rodry's direction. Rodry's air-starved brain grabbed for it, and his fingers closed around the hilt. He slammed the short sword backward, hearing the woman gasp as it went into her, feeling the strangling rope finally give way on his neck.

Rodry scrambled clear of her, back to his feet, rushing over to his sister and hugging her close.

"Rodry!" Lenore said.

"Lenore, are you safe, did they hurt you?" Rodry asked.

"I…" Lenore stood there. "They…" She shook her head. "Are they dead?"

She grabbed for the sword sticking from the man's skull and pulled it clear. The woman was still moving, but only for a moment, because Lenore brought that sword down sharply, hacking into her neck once, then again.

Rodry took the sword from her as gently as she could.

"We need to go," he said. "We need to get home."

"Home?" Lenore said, as if the very idea were hard to take in.

"Come on," Rodry said. "Stay close to me."

He led the way from the room, Lenore following in his wake. The battle was still raging, and even as he watched, Rodry saw a blade plunge into Seris's stomach, his friend striking back with an axe as he fell to bring down one of King Ravin's soldiers. Rodry cut down the next man to step into that space, cutting his way forward through the violence.

"I have her," Rodry yelled out to the others there. "With me!"

His remaining friends formed up around him, as tight as any group of true knights could have been, and Rodry had never been prouder of them than he was in that moment. They fought their way to the door, then out into the sunlight.

A battle was raging around them.

The sergeant and Vars's guards were holding a rough crescent around the door, Rodry and the others' horses within it, waiting. The men there were surrounded by King Ravin's troops, who were limited only by the ditches, which meant that they could only come forward a few at a time, fighting and falling, the screams of the dying horrible to hear.

"We need a way out of this," Rodry said to the sergeant. "We need to get my sister to safety."

"We still have the horses, your highness," the man said. "But there's no path for them. The most my men can do is hold this line, draw their strength. To escape ... you'd have to cut your way through. We could distract them with a charge, but then ..."

Rodry knew without being told how difficult that would be. There were deep ranks of the enemy now, easily enough to bring down horses. To get his sister through all of it seemed impossible. Yet what was the alternative? Surrender? Give her back to King Ravin's men to do with as they wished? He turned to Lenore.

"Can you ride?" he asked.

She hesitated, then nodded. Rodry picked out the strongest of the mounts there, his own, helping Lenore into the saddle. He took Seris's horse, swinging up beside her. Around him, his friends mounted up, while the sergeant's men continued to hold the regiment around the lodge at bay.

"Men!" Rodry called out. "I wish I could say that I was sorry for leading you into this, but the truth is that I would do it a hundred more times if it would save my sister."

"And we'd follow!" Kay called back. He had blood at his side, but he sat straight in the saddle.

"We need to cut our way clear. I'll not lie, it will be far from easy. But we must try! We must be the warriors I know you all to be!"

He'd never been prouder of his friends than as they started to ready lances, sitting tall in the saddle. They formed up in a wedge around Lenore's horse, even though they must all know how dangerous that was.

"We shield the princess," he told them. "We get her to safety. Whatever the cost!"

He turned back to his sister.

"Remember, keep riding, no matter what happens."

"Rodry..."

"I love you, sister," he said.

"I love you too."

"Then keep riding," he insisted. "Get to the bridge. Get to safety."

He turned back to the battle before him. "Sergeant, when you're ready."

The other man nodded. "Men, to me! Charge!"

The guardsmen moved as one, plunging into the enemy, a fist punching into their ranks. Men died in the first rush of that charge, but they cut into the ranks of Ravin's men, slicing so deep into them that for a moment Rodry thought they might scatter them completely.

Then the ranks of King Ravin's soldiers closed around them like a tightening hand, cutting them off. Rodry's instincts were to ride in, to save his men, but he knew that this was the only chance they would get. He saw the ranks of King Ravin's men thinning on the right as they all charged in to take on the guardsmen's attack, and that was an opportunity they could not miss.

"There," Rodry called out, pointing with his sword. "Forward!"

He kicked his horse into a gallop, riding down the first row of the enemy. Beside him, his friends punched into their ranks, lances plunging through foes, swords hacking them down. The sun shone from their armor, and they looked as heroic as any knights out of legend as they fought their way forward.

They cut their way through the ranks of their foes, the goal not to defeat them, but simply to fight their way clear. Rodry cut left and right with his sword, clearing a path almost the way he would have if hacking his way through a forest. It was important not to stop, not to slow. Only getting Lenore to safety mattered now.

The first of his friends fell, Hult, the son of an earl, caught by a spear coming up under his armor. Rodry couldn't even turn and cut down his attacker, had to just keep riding. Greenfell, who was always quick with a joke, went down next, his horse toppling and crushing men even as more poured in to hack at him.

One by one, his friends died, and Rodry felt the ache in his heart of having led them to their deaths, even as he felt pride at what they were doing, at the ground they were making. They shouldn't have been able to cut their way through so many men, even with the distraction of the guards, and yet they were, slicing their way forward step by step, stride by stride, until it seemed that they were just a few yards from freedom.

Looking around, Rodry saw that it was just him, Kay, and Lenore now. He kept going, cutting into the throat of a soldier who got too close, battering away a spear. A sword struck his leg and he ignored it, keeping going, keeping fighting.

Kay charged forward past him, striking a rank of soldiers, riding them down. One grabbed him as he passed, dragging him from his horse. He rose briefly, cutting left and right, opening a path. Then a sword tip seemed to rise up from his chest as a soldier plunged it into his back.

Rodry didn't hesitate, but threw his horse into that last gap, trying to widen it. For a moment, there was a space, and he held that space, turning his horse in place, lashing out at all who got close. He struck down at one soldier, then another. He felt a pain in his side and looked down to see an arrow sticking from it, but he didn't slow, kept fighting.

Lenore was there, level with him now.

Rodry turned to join her, and his horse reared. He saw the spear that plunged into its neck, felt the moment when it went down. Its weight was crushing, but Rodry somehow rolled clear, coming up with his sword already in his hand. He sliced through one soldier's throat, then hacked off the arm of another. He saw Lenore staring at him.

"Go!" he yelled. "Go!"

Pain lanced through him, but Rodry ignored it, cutting down a man who, it turned out, had just stabbed him. Another was there then, and Rodry could feel the weight of his sword now, barely able to lift it as he cut down another foe. He could see Kay on the ground, eyes staring up, mouth moving in silent words as blood poured from him. That distraction cost Rodry as another sword struck him, plunging into his hip. He killed another foe, stumbled and tried to stand.

A dozen men stood around him, spears poised. Rodry didn't care. He rested on one knee for a moment, but didn't stay there. He wouldn't be a prisoner here, wouldn't stop now, when he could buy his sister another few seconds before they started to chase her. He hefted his sword...

He saw the spear that plunged into his chest before it hit him, but he was too weak by then to dodge, too slow. Amazingly, it didn't even hurt. It was just that one moment he was on his feet, and the next, he was on his back, pinned to the mud like an iron moth trapped by a tack. Another spearman stood over him, the weapon aimed at his head.

The last thing Rodry saw was Lenore, riding away, clear of the grasp of those who would hurt her. He'd won. He'd…

Chapter Eighteen

Nerra did her best to settle into life in the refuge. Under Kleos's watchful eyes, she fit in with groups of others like her, helping to prepare food in the kitchens, and chop wood, and clean the compound. She had never been afraid of work.

The others around her seemed to have come from all over the known world. Several were from spots that meant they spoke no language Nerra understood. More had come on boats from the Northern Kingdom, and when they found out who Nerra was, they looked at her strangely.

She could feel the weight of those gazes as she worked at a well, drawing water. A girl stood beside her, twining strands of wool into cord.

"They're just wondering how a disease like this can affect a princess," the girl said. "And how a king would send his daughter to a place like this."

She was probably Nerra's age, a little shorter but broader and stronger, with round, almost heart-shaped features. The scale sickness, *dragon* sickness, Nerra corrected herself, had been particularly cruel with her, not in what it had done, but in what it had left alone. On her left side, this girl was a vision of perfect loveliness, untouched by the marks of the illness. Dark hair fell in waves past her shoulder, while a one-sided smile quirked across her features.

On the other, the black lines of the sickness spread everywhere, leaving only scarred skin on that side of her head, while half of her face was twisted and almost inhuman.

"He didn't send me," Nerra said, thinking of all the things that her father had done to try to save her. He hadn't even been able to bring himself to order her death, the way the law, and his nobles, demanded. "I left myself, and then ... a dragon brought me here."

"A dragon?"

Nerra would have expected most people to scoff at that, or to call her a liar, but most people didn't have the circling forms in the far distance, over the continent.

"I'm Lina," the girl said.

"Nerra," Nerra replied, even though it was clear that the girl knew who she was. "How long have you been here?"

"Since I was little," Lina said. "My parents saw that I had the sickness, and they couldn't bring themselves to ... to kill me, so they brought me here."

"They brought you here and just left you?" Nerra asked. "They haven't come back?"

Lina shook her head. "They send money sometimes, to help Kleos maintain this place. They haven't returned."

Nerra couldn't understand how a parent could do that. Her own parents had done everything they could to help her, to protect her. How could someone just send a child ... here?

"You've been here all your life?" Nerra said. "And you'll stay here until ... until you die?"

It was the kindest way to put it, because what else could Nerra do? Remind Lina that she might transform into a monster, or that Kleos might eventually thrust a knife into her heart?

"Well," Lina said, with a surprising smile. "Unless I go up to the temple fountain to drink the waters, of course."

She laughed as if it were a joke.

Nerra stared at her. "I don't understand."

"No one has told you about the temple waters?" Lina said. "It's an old story here. There's a temple up on the far side of the volcano." She nodded to the peaks that dominated the island. "There's a fountain there whose waters are supposed to be able to cure the sickness."

She said it casually, as if it were nothing, but the words struck inside Nerra like a hammer.

"There's a cure?" she asked, her eyes going wide.

"Oh." Lina's expression instantly became one of concern, her hands going to Nerra's shoulders. "Nerra, it's a story, a rumor. People go and try, but when I asked Kleos, he told me that it wasn't real."

Nerra felt her hopes deflate a little. Even so, she knew that she couldn't let this go. She had to know the truth about the waters. She had to ask Kleos.

⚜ ⚜ ⚜

Nerra found Kleos in a simple wooden hut that seemed to be his own. There was no ostentation here, no display, barely anything at all beyond a bed, a table, and a mat on which Kleos knelt, apparently deep in prayer or thought.

Nerra waited for him to finish, standing in the doorway, trying to remain patient in spite of what she'd heard. Her hands clenched and unclenched, working with the urge to rush forward and grab him by the shoulder. She forced herself to stay still and wait with an effort.

"Yes, Nerra?" Kleos said, without turning round.

"Tell me about the temple fountain," Nerra said.

She heard the older man sigh. "You've heard that story, then."

"Lina mentioned it," Nerra said.

Kleos turned to her, looking at her with pity, but also with a kind of determination. "And now you're wondering why I am not sending everyone here to drink those waters?"

"I... yes," Nerra admitted. If something like that existed, why wouldn't everyone know? Why weren't all those like her being sent to be cured?

"Because the story is not true," Kleos said. "There is a temple, and there are waters, but those waters are not a cure."

"But why?" Nerra said. "Why is there even a story?"

Kleos moved back to sit at the table there. "It is hard to be sure," he said. "It is said that the temple was once intended to be an attempt to cure the sickness, back in the days when dragons were more common outside of Sarrass. It is even said that it worked, although I am not sure if I believe that. I *do* know that the waters were cursed."

"Cursed?" Nerra said. "You don't believe in healing waters, but you believe in curses?"

"I've seen enough evidence of this one," Kleos said. "The waters are death, Nerra. I have seen dozens, hundreds, try them. All have died."

"So they're poisoned?" Nerra asked. Instantly, she found herself thinking of the herbs she knew so much about, and the ways the world held to counter poisons.

"Not poisoned, cursed," Kleos said. He sighed again. "These are stories out of the oldest days, half-remembered things. Some say that dragons ruled in those days, or those who sided with them, it is not clear. Some say that the Slate River only exists because of dragon fire in the wars to be rid of that rule. Those were days of things that could not happen now."

"Like a fountain to cure the sickness, and a curse to stop it working?" Nerra said.

Kleos nodded. "The stories say that a sorcerer worked magic on it. That he proclaimed that those who drank would die mad, twisted, torn apart."

Nerra paused, considering those words.

"And now you're wondering if the cure might be worth the risk," Kleos said. He shook his head. "Believe me, girl, there's no cure."

"How can you be so sure?" Nerra asked.

"Because I've seen all the *others* who were certain that they would survive," Kleos snapped back. "Do you think that everyone else doesn't think they might be special, that they might be the one to break the chain of endless death? They go, one after another. Many of them die on the way, because that way is *hard*."

"And the ones who don't?" Nerra asked. She had to hear it.

"They drink, and they die," Kleos said. "Their bodies twist into horrific things, and their minds are worse by the end. They die screaming and raging, their own bodies turned into weapons against them. The same way you will die if you try this."

He made it sound as certain as the sun rising.

"So what am I supposed to do?" Nerra asked. "Just sit here and wait to change so much that you kill me?"

"You're meant to live out your life," Kleos said. "To make the most of the limited time that you still have. To prepare yourself for what will, inevitably, come." He paused for a few seconds. "Do you want to know what I believe about the temple? I believe that the stories of a cure were created for those who could not do that, for the ones who couldn't find peace. I think the fountain was put there as a way out for them, as a way to think they were helping themselves even while they died. Do not be so foolish. You still have time; live in it."

Live in it. That was easy to say when Kleos didn't have the sickness that the rest of them had. When he was the one who killed them when they changed too far. Did he enjoy that part? Would he enjoy cutting Nerra's throat when the time came?

"Promise me," Kleos said. "Promise me that you won't seek out the temple."

"I promise," Nerra said, but even as she did so, she knew she was lying.

Chapter Nineteen

As she and Odd came into sight of the largest bridge to the south, Erin barely slowed. She raced toward it, Odd's mule struggling to keep up in the wake of her horse. She charged down toward the bridge, and it was only as she reached it that she slowed, stopped, dismounted.

Dead men lay around the start of the bridge's span, wearing the uniforms of her family's men, clearly cut down before they could react. Erin stared down at them, wondering what it must have been like for them to be cut down so suddenly.

"They came this way then," Odd said, dropping down from his mule. "There are more tracks, too. A second force went this way afterwards."

He pointed, and Erin could see what he meant. Although with one of the great bridges, it was hard to truly tell when people had gone across. Erin was more interested in the fact that Odd could pick apart the tracks so easily. He'd mentioned being a former knight, but Erin still didn't have the first clue who he was. He was just... Odd.

"We need to cross," Erin said.

Odd nodded. "If that's where your sister is, that's where we have to go."

Erin frowned at that. "No speech about how this is too dangerous, or about how angry the king will be if his knights start raiding across the bridges and start a war?"

"War is coming anyway," Odd said. "And I... I have a poor record of listening to those I should."

He set out over the bridge on foot, leading his by now exhausted mule. He paused by one of the slain guards, closing his staring eyes, but also lifting the man's short bow and a quiver of arrows. Taking her cue from him, Erin did the same with a crossbow.

"A real bow is better," Odd said. "Crossbows hit harder, but an archer with the skill to do it can send six arrows flying for every bolt they fire."

"A crossbow is what's here," Erin pointed out. Did this strange man think he was her teacher now?

"True," Odd said, and kept going across the bridge's broad span.

Erin had never been across the Slate before. The bridge between its shores was wide enough that it seemed to take an age to walk it, its wooden slats creaking beneath her feet. She supposed that she should have felt some security in that instability, in the power of the Slate to keep the two kingdoms apart. Yet, from what Odd had said, even that wasn't enough anymore.

Who *was* this man who was not a knight, or a monk, but both and less all at once?

There was no answer to that, so Erin kept leading her horse. She was most of the way across when she saw figures emerge from the trees on the far shore. There was a chasing cluster of horsemen, dressed in the colors of King Ravin, but Erin was more interested in the figure riding out in front of them, racing ahead of the chasing pack for her life.

"Lenore!" Erin called out. It was too far for her sister to hear her, but Erin shouted it anyway. She started forward toward her sister, horse moving at a flat run now, Odd following in her wake.

The distance between them closed quickly. Erin could see every detail of her sister's face, see the fear there, but also the determination. She saw one of the chasing pack of riders getting closer, breaking from the pack. She raised her crossbow and fired it, saw the bolt arc out and slam into the man's chest. He toppled, and Erin kept riding.

She reached Lenore and wheeled her horse, all three stopping for a second. Lenore was staring at her, in obvious shock that her sister was there, but where else in the world would Erin be when Lenore was in danger?

"Erin? How… how are you here?" Lenore asked.

"I'm here to help you," Erin said.

Beside her, Odd raised his bow. He fired once, nocked another arrow, then fired again. Horses toppled among the chasing pack.

"We need to go," he said. "Reunions later."

"We could hold here," Erin said. "Give Lenore time to—"

"*No,*" Lenore said. "That's what Rodry did!"

"Rodry?" Erin said.

"Rodry…" Lenore looked pale, shaking her head in grief. "He came to save me. He fought to get me out, and…he's dead, Erin. He's dead."

Grief hit Erin like a punch to the stomach. She felt as though she might fall from the saddle, the whole world starting to curl inward around her. She sat there blankly, not comprehending…

Then Odd slapped the side of her helmet, hard enough to make it ring. "There is no *time* for this," he yelled at her. "No time for grief, no time for hesitation. No time even for me to ask why your entire family seems to have the names of King Godwin's children! We need to *go.*"

Erin nodded, and wheeled her horse back toward the bridge, alongside Lenore and Odd. They galloped at full pelt, but a single glance back over her shoulder told her that the men there were closing, even though they were almost at the bridge. Erin could feel the slats of the bridge under her horse's hooves now, but the men didn't stop. One was ahead of the others, an axe raised…

Odd was there, sword in hand, intercepting it and knocking the man from his saddle, off into the waters below. Erin saw Odd leap down, letting his mule keep running.

"We need to face them," he called. "We can't run fast enough over the bridge. They'll just cut us down."

Erin dropped down beside him, onto the slats of the bridge, turning to face the onrush of enemies.

"At least you didn't tell me to keep running," Erin said, as she readied her spear.

"And face all those alone?" Odd countered, nodding to the horsemen approaching, slowing as they came to the bridge. "I might be called mad, but I'm not *stupid.*"

Erin looked at the group there. There had to be twenty of them, but the bridge was narrow enough that only a few of them would be able to fit onto the bridge side by side to fight.

"How do we do this?" Erin asked.

Odd frowned at her. "What's to understand? We fight them, we kill them, we back away step by step until we cross this thrice damned bridge."

Erin looked at the slow advance of the men there. "Why aren't they coming faster?"

Odd shrugged. "No one wants to die first."

That didn't last long though. The riders came forward, the first of them obviously confident that they could ride down a girl and a monk with ease. He swung at Erin and she turned the blow away, thrusting up with her spear into his ribs and toppling him into the waters beyond the bridge.

Another was already striking at Odd. He swayed back from the cut, dragged the man from his saddle, and killed him with a downward thrust of his sword before backing away a few more paces.

They came on foot then, obviously realizing that without the advantage of space, horses wouldn't work. They came in tight formation, three wide, thrusting and cutting with swords and spears while Erin and Odd gave ground.

Erin blocked one blow, kicked at a man's knee and stepped back. Odd hacked a man's head from his shoulders, pushed another by his shield into the water. Erin caught another blow that was aimed at his heart as he did it, and he grinned at her before cutting open a soldier's throat.

Erin glanced back to see how Lenore was escaping. She saw her sister waiting at the far shore now, clear of the fight but making no move to keep moving further back. She clearly wasn't going to just run and leave them—

Odd caught a sword blow just in front of her face. "Focus! Unless you want to lose your head?"

Erin stabbed another of the attacking troops in answer. It was getting worse now, because she could see a whole cluster of infantry coming in from the trees now, too many to ever fight. All she and Odd could do was keep killing, and keep giving ground.

Odd fought with speed and power, but also a seeming lack of care. He didn't hide behind his defenses like many warriors, but threw himself into cuts like a whirlwind. Erin found herself fitting into the rhythm of his attacks, striking in the spaces that he left, trying to cover any openings. Her armor protected her as a sword glanced from it, her buckler took a blow from an axe. Both of them took wounds though. Erin felt the impact of every blow that landed, even if her armor stopped her from being cut in half. Odd seemed to be bleeding from a dozen places, even though at least that many men lay dead in his wake.

They both gave ground, step by step. They were running out of ground to give, though. It should have been a good thing that they were getting closer and closer to the Northern Kingdom's shore, closer to home, and to safety. The problem was that, for now, the *bridge* was safety. The bridge was the thing that meant that the soldiers before Erin and Odd couldn't surround them, couldn't spread out and overwhelm them with their numbers.

"We're running out of room," Erin said, with a nervous glance back at the end of the bridge.

"So we hold them back at the edge of the bridge and kill all of them," Odd said, as if it were the easiest thing in the world. Did he actually believe that? Did he actually think that they could stand there and kill King Ravin's armies one by one?

Erin didn't. She knew that when they reached the end of the bridge, it would be done. She still fought, still killed. She slashed the head of her spear across a man's leg, thrust the point up into another's skull. The stroke of an axe jarred her as she blocked it, but she kept going.

They couldn't hold, though. They would reach the end of the bridge, and then...then, no matter how hard they fought, the sheer weight of men would push them back another few steps. It would mean being surrounded, blades coming from every side...

That was when Erin heard the horns behind her. She thrust her spear into a man's gut, swept it round to clear a space for her to glance round, and she dared to look...

Her father's army stood there. There were knights there, and guardsmen, and more. There were archers, who even now were readying arrows to fire down into the ranks of the men on the bridge. There were horsemen standing by, ready to charge. Her father sat at the heart of it all, looking mighty in his armor, unconquerable. Erin couldn't count the numbers compared to the force that had followed Lenore, and was now struggling to cross the bridge, but it was close, so close...

Horns sounded again, and her father's army charged.

Chapter Twenty

King Godwin advanced with the bulk of his army, men drawn from around the kingdom descending on the bridge below. The other bridges would be fallen now, torn down in accordance with his commands.

The one below... he would command that destroyed too, if he could. The mechanism to do it was there: the pegs in place that could be hammered out, letting crucial poles slide out of place, with the weight of the bridge doing the rest. The whole *point* of the bridges was that they could be torn away to protect the kingdom.

Yet now, there was no way to do that; not with one of his daughters standing by the bridge, another on it, and his son Rodry somewhere across it. In circumstances like those, even with King Ravin's armies there upon the span, even with more and still more pouring in on the far bank, until it seemed that it was flooded with hundreds of men, there was only one thing to do.

"Charge!" he commanded. "Hold the bank!"

His knights leapt to obey his commands, Twell and Ursus, Halfin and Lors moving down at the head of a wave of his troops. Godwin charged with them, praying that he would be in time.

Already, he could see the bank being breached, Erin and the strange man in the monk's robes pushed back that one crucial step to let men through. The soldiers spread out around them, and for a moment, Godwin's heart clamped tight in his chest at the thought that he might lose both Erin and Lenore in one moment. If the soldiers formed a true beachhead, then there might be no stopping them.

Godwin saw his men slam into the enemy, though, the weight of their numbers pressing in, smashing that beachhead back, cutting off those who had made it to the far side, a wave of armored bodies slamming into their line. Godwin saw Ursus pick up a man and throw him into the Slate, saw Halfin dodge past a spear and slice through a man's shoulder.

In that moment, his knights were everything that they had ever been. Godwin saw Commander Harr and his men join the fray, pressing King Ravin's soldiers back, forcing them almost halfway over the bridge. The bridge creaked with the weight of so many men on it, its narrowness crushing them together, leaving only a little room to swing a weapon. On the bank, there was more space, but even that was quickly filled up with men fighting and dying.

Then Godwin was in the battle himself, charging into those of King Ravin's soldiers who were still on the bank, determined to fight his way to the spot where Lenore still sat atop her horse. He took the blow of an axe on his shield, sliced through a man's leg, used his elbow to barge another man aside. He took a blow to his armor, but it made no difference, didn't even slow him.

Not by the hand you think. Grey's words ran through his mind and Godwin looked around, seeing a spearman charging at him from the side. He struck the spear aside, and then Sir Lors was there, his two swords swinging to bring the spearman down.

"So much for your prophecy, wizard!" Godwin shouted out above the roar of the battle.

No one was listening. Around him, men were pushing and shoving, cutting and killing, the confines of the bridge taking away all room for tactics, all the space that might have provided the chance for some clever ruse or careful plan. There was only the press of the melee, the small fights against those who broke through onto the near bank, and the endless violence of it all.

Even as he thought it, Godwin fought his way forward. He lanced his sword through another soldier's chest, kicked a second man out of the way. A sword caught him across the side, but the wound was not a deep one, and beside him, Sir Lors was already moving to kill the man. Both swords plunged into him, meeting somewhere in the middle.

Then the soldier grabbed for him as he died.

"Back!" Godwin yelled at the knight, and ten years ago, the man might have been fast enough to do it.

Now though, the soldier got a hold on him, clinging to him as he died, and *that* slowed the knight enough that another man could step in, a sword slamming into his neck. Godwin stepped close with a cry of anger, cutting that soldier down, but there was nothing he could do to help Sir Lors, and no time in which to do it. He had to keep fighting his way toward his daughters.

He saw Erin in the press of the fight, the strange monk still beside her, the two fighting like two parts of a whole, killing King Ravin's troops as they came. Godwin was proud of his daughter in that moment, but also scared for her, caught in the middle of the battle like that. Even as he watched, a spearman came at her, but Commander Harr was there, cutting down the man and holding back the enemy for a moment while Erin slipped by, striking out with her own short weapon.

He was just as frightened for Lenore, whose horse was whirling back and forth in the middle of the press of men there. Why hadn't she run from the bridge to safety? Godwin didn't know, but he was going to get to her. He forced his way forward, cutting down men to either side, trying to force a gap to open. Sir Twell was there then, holding the line beside him, seeming to see what was needed. His shoulder was bleeding from a sword wound, but he held his place, while Godwin fought his way forward, cutting down a man who was too close to his daughter's horse, reaching up to clasp her hand in his.

They'd done it. They'd gotten to her. Now, they just had to get her home safely, and *that* was still going to be far from easy, when the battle was still raging on every side.

⚜ ⚜ ⚜

From his vantage point away from the bridge, hiding behind a low tree stump, Vars watched the battle starting to unfold. He crouched there and he stared, taking in the violence of the battle, the men fighting and dying on the span of the bridge stretching into the distance, over to the south.

He saw Erin killing men with that twig-like spear of hers, saw Lenore there on her horse, saw his father fighting his way to her.

He saw men falling, on both sides. A knight went down with a halberd embedded deep in him. King Ravin's soldiers fell from the bridge like scarlet-coated rain, dropping to sword blows or simply being thrown from it.

He wanted to go down to help, even though Vars couldn't understand why men would risk themselves like that, why they would throw themselves into a battle where there was no way to avoid the foe, no way to keep back from the blows that fell in a cascade. His father stood at the heart of the fighting, directing it even as he fought, in a way that simply made no sense to Vars.

He wanted to throw himself into the thick of it, even ordered his legs to carry him forward, but they wouldn't move. They refused, the way a horse might refuse to jump a wall. He ... he simply couldn't do it.

Which just left the question of what he was going to do. Did he stand there, and risk someone seeing him there, hanging back from the battle? Clearly he couldn't do that. If his father knew that he was there and not lending the strength of his arm, he would be treated as a coward, or worse, a traitor.

Did he throw himself into the battle then, to let people see him in the thick of the fight? That seemed almost as stupid. Even if Vars stuck to the edges of the fighting, there was too much of a risk of a stray sword blow catching him, a thrown spear or a sudden arrow bringing him down. Worse, it would raise far too many questions about why Vars hadn't been there before.

He tried to work out what he was going to do about that. If Lenore had been lost completely, he could have made up any story he pleased, claimed that he had fought hard to save her. Now, he would need to think of another way to do things.

About the only positive note was that there was no sign of Rodry, or of the men who had ridden off with him, betraying Vars to hurry blindly into the enemy's lands. Vars felt a small pang of regret at that, at the thought that his brother might be lost completely, but that pang was short lived, and not just because Vars could still feel the bruise from where his brother had struck him.

If Rodry was gone, it was down to his own stupidity. It was because he hadn't listened to Vars, hadn't listened to *sense.* Vars had told him that no good could come of charging across the river. Now, for all those who had gone, only Lenore, Erin, and the strange monk had returned. None of them could say what Vars had and hadn't done.

As far as they were concerned, he had never been here. If he left now, no one could say that he hadn't been attacked on the road, ambushed before he reached Lenore. If she disagreed, well... Vars would deal with that when it came.

For now, he was safest well clear of this fight. That much was obvious. So, while the battle raged behind him, Vars very quickly, very quietly, slipped away and started back toward Royalsport.

Chapter Twenty One

Odd was slowly falling out of his battle rage. Oh, he *tried* to maintain it, tried to froth and shout and throw himself blindly at the enemy, but his heart wasn't in it in quite the same way that it used to be. That didn't stop him from battering aside a shield, hacking the top of a skull from the rest, but even so, he could feel the fire within him dimming.

Part of it had to do with the many small wounds he'd sustained so far in the battle on the bridge. You could say what you liked about plate armor, but at least it stopped scratches like the one that ran all the way down his forearm now.

Part of it seemed to have to do with the presence of the girl by his side. She fought with her own kind of anger, which seemed more focused, but less completely trained than his. Odd found himself moving across to protect her from sword blows when they came at her, interposing steel in a way he usually didn't. Normally, his battle madness left him little sense that anyone was on his side, let alone the urge to protect them. With Erin, it seemed to be different, and not just because Odd had worked out *exactly* who this girl had to be when the king came running for her and her sister.

Part of it, though, was that there was something deeper there, something that felt almost *peaceful,* in a way nothing had a right to be in the middle of a battle like this. Beside him, a guardsman had his ribs shattered by a hammer, a knight fell into the waters where his armor would only drag him down. Instead of his usual furious laughter, though, Odd smiled beatifically. It all fit. It all made *sense,* and in doing so, it felt beautiful.

That didn't stop him from punching his sword through an enemy's gorget, or smashing the pommel into another's skull. Those things were as much a part of the meditation as the rest of it. Odd kept fighting, and around him on the bridge, the world turned into the most beautiful hell he had ever seen.

⚜ ⚜ ⚜

Erin forced herself to stay in the heart of the battle, refusing to pull back even though she was sure that half of those there would have liked to see her safe back behind the lines. She thrust with her spear, spun it in a distraction, used it to trip a man's legs from under him. Here at the edge of the bridge, everything was chaos, with no neat lines now, no sense of which direction the next sword blow might come from. Anyone might be a friend or a—

"Look out!"

Erin ducked on instinct, and a sword blow went flashing above her head. She thrust backward with her spear, feeling the crunch as it entered flesh, then let the soldier she'd just stabbed fall.

She looked round to see Commander Harr standing in the midst of the battle, swinging a great sword with ease. Erin had seen him on the practice field, but this was something different, something deadlier. He frowned at her presence in a way that said that there would be consequences for running out ahead the way she had, but right then there was no time for Erin to think about any of that, only to parry and thrust, throwing herself back into the action...

⚜ ⚜ ⚜

Commander Harr was feeling his age. Around him, he could see men he'd served with for decades in the Knights of the Spur throwing themselves into the fray like young men, but he was anything but young these days. He had to fight carefully instead, conserving his energy, measuring each swing of his blade the way a carpenter might have measured prior to a cut.

He shortened one foe by a head in a single sweep, moved back to avoid a blow, then felt the pain of a dagger finding one of the seams of his armor. Commander Harr bellowed at that, because even a decade ago, no one would have gotten close enough to inflict such a wound. He lashed out in reply, all but cutting the foe who had closed with him in two, then ripped the dagger clear with a grunt of effort.

His eyes found Erin. She fought as he had thought that she might from the training grounds, with speed and skill, but also with a dangerous touch of recklessness. Three times now, he'd seen the man beside her parry blows aimed at her, his monk's robes flowing as he did it.

Of course, Commander Harr knew that was no monk. There were some faces that even time could not erase, from memory, some sights that were too heavily etched to be unseen. The way this "monk" danced through the fight even within the horrific press of the bridge was a kind of signature in itself, yet there was something different about it too.

There was no time to consider that though, because the battle was still washing back and forth on the bridge, the press of it too great. Worse, Commander Harr could see still more troops pouring in from the Southern Kingdom's side. How many could there be? More importantly, how could even the Knights of the Spur hope to hold against so many? Even as he watched, men tumbled from the bridge, one man hanging from another's grasp on the very edge.

Commander Harr shook away that thought. It didn't matter how many there were; only that they kept fighting. He plunged back toward the fight.

⚜ ⚜ ⚜

"We're getting too old for this!" Sir Halfin yelled up, as he hung over the edge of the bridge, held only by Sir Ursus's grasp.

"You're getting too *fat* for it!" Ursus yelled back, and that was probably a good sign. The big man wouldn't be making jokes about it if he didn't feel certain that he could pull Halfin back onto the bridge. At least, he hoped not.

"Just pull me up!" Halfin called out. Hanging above the Slate was *not* where he wanted to be, not with the river raging below him, and the drop enough in itself that it might kill someone.

How had he gotten into this spot? He'd been charging forward, throwing himself through the fight, and then a man had come at him and ... and he hadn't been fast enough to dodge.

He, Halfin the Swift, hadn't been fast enough. That was a humbling thought, a reminder that all of those who had served the king loyally for so long, were getting older. There were some younger knights, Prince Rodry foremost among them, but the truth was that Halfin and Ursus and the rest were getting past their best. He just had to hope that this wouldn't be a battle too far for them.

Then Sir Ursus gave a roar of pain, and the head of a spear appeared, thrust through his shoulder from the rear. He bellowed like a wounded bull, and for a moment, Halfin was sure that he was going to drop. Instead though, Sir Ursus roared again, this time with effort, and Halfin found himself being lifted as easily as the other knight had always been able to lift him, throwing him back onto the bridge. Sir Halfin landed lightly as an acrobat, thrusting with his sword as he landed, bringing down the man who had wounded his friend.

He moved to prop up Sir Ursus, the weight of the larger knight almost enough to squash him. In spite of that, Sir Halfin was still able to cut out again, bringing down another of the enemy.

Maybe they weren't quite done yet.

⚜ ⚜ ⚜

At the heart of it all on the bank, Lenore sat atop her horse, forcing herself to be brave, to not move. She fought to contain the skittishness of the creature, because if it bolted now, there was a good chance that it might plunge her down into the waters between the kingdom.

Around her, men died, blood spraying, the world filled with the clash of steel and the screams of the dying. To her side, the horrendous drop down to the Slate stood, the banks crumbling a little under the weight of so many men stomping and fighting, pushing and pulling at the edge of it. She saw a man's leg hacked off a few feet away, saw another shoved off the edge of the cliff down into the river. A part of her longed to run, but she couldn't bring herself to do that, not when her sister was still out there on the bridge, fighting to hold back the tide of enemies.

What would happen if she died here? With so much violence on every side, how could she hope to survive? Fear wormed through her there.

What if she'd gone through all of this, if Rodry had sacrificed himself, and Erin had journeyed to the south, just so that she could die in the chaos of the battle that followed?

Only the fact that she was obviously not a soldier seemed to be keeping Lenore safe right then; that, and the presence of so many of her father's men around her, shielding her with their efforts, killing those who came too close. Her father was there too, huge and armored, and he seemed the comforting presence that he had always been, strong and safe, impossible to defeat.

Yet one look at the bridge told Lenore how fragile that illusion was. She could see it swaying under the weight of so many men, could hear the creaking of it even above the sounds of the dying. She had felt for herself that no one was truly safe, that men of violence could always find a way to hurt, to kill, to do worse...

There were more men on the bridge than she could count, more still approaching it, mere dots in the distance, given the Slate's width. Even on this bank, there were dozens of pockets of them, spread out and fighting, attacking her father's men from all sides. How could even her father hope to hold against all that? How could any of them? The battle kept going, but in that moment, Lenore couldn't see how they could hope to win it.

Chapter Twenty Two

King Godwin stood at the heart of the battle, holding onto his daughter's horse and trying to make sense of it all. *That* was the most important skill for a war leader; not the ability to wade into the fight, not the ability to inspire men, although both mattered. The ability to step back for a second and just *look* counted for more than the rest of it put together.

"Are you safe?" he bellowed to Lenore, even over the sounds of the battle.

"I…" She nodded, but there was something about the way that she did it that spoke of pains that she couldn't voice, not there.

A man came at Godwin in that moment, and for a second, everything was the violence. He smashed the man back, fought his way back to Lenore's skittish horse, managed to catch hold of it again.

"And what about your brother?" he asked. "Have you seen Rodry?"

This look said almost as much as the last one, and it hurt just as sharply.

"He… he came to save me," she said. "They killed him, Father. Rodry is dead."

If he'd been anywhere but a battle, King Godwin would have collapsed to the ground in grief at the news. Even so, the hurt of it burned through him, making him roar out his grief, lash out at the first enemy to come near.

"My son!" he bellowed, as he struck down a man. "You killed my *son*!"

He killed then, one man after another. His knights formed around him, but even like that, it was hard for them to keep up as he thrust his sword through one man, then hacked down the next.

Step back, he told himself, the voice of his reason trying to cut through his grief, *step back*.

He did it then, shoving back the nearest of his enemies and standing in the clear space that the movement left, staring out over the battle through tear-clouded eyes. He would be strong, *had* to be strong. He would look at this like a commander, and a king, because to look like a father was to lose everything. Godwin stood there, his heart breaking, and around him, the rhythms of the battle kept on.

He saw the fight on the bridge continuing, the press of men there shoving back and forth to no avail. It wasn't that King Ravin's forces were pushing them back yet, although if numbers continued to pour in from their side, the sheer weight of them might force his army back onto the Northern Kingdom's lands, might leave them running or dying. The parts that worried Godwin more…

There were two. One was that he and his men simply couldn't win this fight. Even if they somehow fought their way to the far side of the bridge, the Southern Kingdom's forces could hold his army as easily as he could hold theirs. The best that they could hope for was to fight to a standstill.

The worse fear was for his daughters. He'd lost so much in such a short time, with Nerra gone, Lenore taken, Rodry… Godwin let out a cry of anguish, cast his sword down, and smashed a man aside with his shield instead. No more. He would allow no more of his children to suffer.

"Sound the withdrawal," he ordered, yelling it out over the battle. "Pull back and hold our side. Not a foot on the bridge!"

His men started to pull back, and Godwin turned to the knights around him. He found Twell, found Bolis.

"Help me collapse the bridge," he commanded. "We left it standing to get my daughter back. Now… I want it down!"

"Yes, your majesty," the men chorused, and fought their way forward, through the press. Godwin went with them, snatching up a war hammer from a fallen foe. He struck with it at a man's helm, parried a blow on his shield, continued to fight his way on.

Out on the bridge, his forces started to pull back. The ordinary men ran for safety, but the Knights of the Spur fought while backing away, giving ground but never exposing their backs. It meant that, where another force might have been cut down in a rout, they were able to withdraw in good order. Godwin saw his daughter and the strange monk among them, leapfrogging one another as they pulled back again to the very edge of the bridge.

Ahead of him, he saw Twell and Bolis fighting to get to the wooden pegs that held the bridge in place. Godwin saw Bolis duck under a blow, only to trip as a body caught his foot. He fell, and a sword came down, too quick to stop. Godwin killed the attacker himself, bringing the war hammer around in a wicked arc that ended in a crunch of bone.

Twell was there, staring down at his fallen comrade. Godwin strode to him, shaking him by the shoulders.

"How do we do this?" Godwin demanded of the knight who was still standing. "You know these things. Where do we strike, Planner?"

He knew what it was like to feel the shock of someone being taken away. He could feel it running through his blood now at the thought that his son was gone. The only way to stop that from consuming everything though was to keep going, to win this fight.

"Where?" he demanded, and Twell pointed. Godwin saw the holding pegs then, smaller than he would have thought they might be to hold so much. Now that the knight had pointed it out though, he could see the way the structure held together, one part holding another, the whole linking together in one interconnected tangle of wood and iron.

He ran to the spot, using his shield to barge a man into the Slate below. He stood there for a moment, watching his troops pull back from the bridge. He saw Commander Harr step from it, saw the strange monk slide away, saw Erin...

A soldier grabbed her, hanging onto her as if he might pull her back onto the bridge. Godwin took a step, as if he might go to fetch her himself, but he didn't need to. The man in the monk's robes was there, pulling her away from her foe and cutting him down. Together, they leapt from the bridge.

Godwin struck, hammer slamming down on the peg once, then again. He felt it give, felt it shift. Beside him, Twell cut down a man who came at him to try to stop him. Godwin struck a third blow, hard enough to ring out above the battle.

The peg gave way, tumbling into the water below.

For a moment, Godwin thought that nothing had happened; that Twell the Planner had misjudged it, age catching up with his cunning as it had others' strength or speed. Then he saw the bridge shift, and twist, and start to tumble.

It came apart like the fall of leaves from an autumn tree, except that every leaf was a span of wood larger than a man. There were men too, in that fall, each one screaming as they tumbled, the red of Ravin's colors filling the sky as they fell to the enveloping gray waters of the Slate. There was blue among them too, because some men had been so deep on the bridge that there was no chance for them. Godwin stared at those specks, thinking of his son, and all the other fathers who would know the pain he was feeling now.

Around him, the battle continued, but it was a losing thing now for those of Ravin's men who were on this side of the bridge. There were too few of them to hope to achieve victory, too few to do anything but fall to his knights, or offer themselves in surrender.

One man came at him, charging with a blade ready in his hand. Godwin stepped in to meet him, shield raised...

And that was when a second man, dressed in scraps of armor that had obviously been stolen from dead men, stepped in close, jabbing a knife into Godwin's side.

"King Ravin thought you would come for your daughter," he whispered. "So he told me to be ready."

Godwin didn't answer, but turned, lifting the man bodily. The king hauled him over his head, and then flung him, over the edge, into the river with the others. Even as he was doing it, Twell cut down the one who had come from the front. Godwin turned to congratulate the knight, then found himself falling, caught only because Sir Twell was there to interpose himself.

Godwin felt something throbbing in his side, the world closing in around him. He couldn't move then, couldn't speak, couldn't blink. The knife...there had been something on the knife...

"The king!" Sir Twell called out. "The king has fallen!"

Chapter Twenty Three

Greave had never been more grateful than when the Serpentine finally drew to a halt outside Astare, the ship bumping up against a narrow quay a little way from the city. Only a few other boats sat in the harbor, mostly fishing vessels and an occasional small merchant cog. The Northern Kingdom was not a place that valued the sea; having seen its dangers, Greave was starting to understand why.

"We're here," Aurelle breathed beside him. "We're actually here."

She sounded worried by that, as if certain that things wouldn't be so easy, or as if some other problem was about to loom. Greave couldn't blame her for that, after everything that had happened. He put a comforting hand on her shoulder.

"Everything will be all right," he promised her.

"Because you will stand and protect me against whatever dangers this part of your father's kingdom holds?" Aurelle asked.

"I would," Greave said. "In a heartbeat."

The briefest look of surprise crossed Aurelle's face, there and gone again in a flash. She must have known after the attack by the darkmaw that he would risk himself for her, but then, this was a cruel world. Maybe it was hard to believe that someone like Greave *could* stand against danger. He was hardly his brother Rodry, to kill any who threatened his love.

His love ... when had he started thinking of Aurelle as that? Long enough ago that Greave couldn't even remember when he'd started.

"I am so grateful that you came with me," he said, holding onto Aurelle tightly. "It means more than I can say that you would choose to be by my side."

"Where else would I be?" Aurelle asked. "This…this is where I'm meant to be."

Again, Greave felt his heart swell with love he hadn't known was possible until he met her. He looked up at the city, which sat at the top of a path from this small harbor, reached by flights of steps that wound their way up, moving back and forth. From here, he could see gray granite walls around some of the city, the spires of towers poking up above like the fingers of some gigantic stone hand. One of them would be the library.

"We need to hurry," Greave said. "The sooner we get there, the sooner we can find a cure for Nerra."

He had to believe that there was such a thing hidden away there; that his sister could be helped. He grabbed his belongings and stepped down from the ship. Instantly, the world seemed to sway. Aurelle tumbled against him, but seemed to catch herself with perfect grace.

"What is this?" she asked.

"The writer Yarrin suggests that our bodies become accustomed to the movement of ships," Greave said, "so that on land again, it seems to be moving for several minutes. He posits the idea of a fluid filled sac in the inner ear that…" It occurred to him that he was lecturing her. "Sorry."

"You don't need to stop," Aurelle said. "Being interested in the world is part of what makes you who you are."

They set off together, arm in arm only partly for the stability it provided, making their way up the long staircase that led to the city. Eventually, Astare stood before them. Some of it had sprawled beyond its walls, in the way of cities, low wooden houses spread out in a scattering along the sides of roads leading south and east, shops and workshops spread out among them so that the exterior of the walls seemed busier than the interior. There was only so far that the outer city could spread though, because hills stood around it in a second kind of wall, cut through by passes.

Greave's attention was on the inner city and its towers, though. They stretched up into the heavens, built from gray stone and capped with red terracotta roofs. Each seemed so elegant, so finely constructed, clearly belonging to a scholar of the House of Scholars, or to those who employed them. One would be the great library, it had to be.

He strode to the gate between the outer city and the inner. It was open, but the difference between the two was clear. Outside, the roads were dirt, the houses low and mud stained. Inside, every road was cobbled, every house constructed as if to some master plan that had been set out for the whole, fitting together in neat grids and squares clustered around open, green spaces. It was beautiful and orderly at once, a contrast to the river cut chaos of Royalsport.

"Move along," a guard at the gate said.

"This is your prince, Prince Greave," Aurelle replied.

The guard looked at Greave, paused, and then laughed. "Of course he is. And I'm the king himself."

It occurred to Greave that after his time at sea, he probably didn't look as refined as he had. His clothes were salt stained, and his hair disheveled. Aurelle looked as though she might argue with the guard, but Greave put a hand on her arm.

"It's all right," he said. "We don't want them barring us from entry."

For a second, Greave thought that she might argue anyway, but she seemed to catch his worried expression and relent.

"Which way to the Great Library?" Greave asked.

The guard laughed again. "Your servants didn't tell you, 'your highness'? Just go to the main square. The tower is right at the center of the city."

Greave hurried into the city as the guard stepped back. Aurelle caught his arm.

"Can we at least find an inn first?" she asked. "If even the guards think that you're some vagrant, what will the House of Scholars do?"

"I…" Greave wanted to act, wanted to save his sister from her illness *now*, but he knew Aurelle was right. It was late afternoon, and they'd just gotten off the boat. They needed to rest.

They took a room at a small inn that seemed to be almost perfectly round and made of dark stone, constructed as if as a technical exercise by architects of the House of Scholars. The innkeeper looked at them as if they might rob the place until Greave put money down on the bar for a room, food, a bath. Aurelle led him up the stairs of the place laughing, and if she stumbled against him this time as they reached their room, it had nothing to do with her sea legs.

⚜ ⚜ ⚜

In the morning, Greave made himself as presentable as he could, digging out a fresh shirt, tunic, and hose of dark silk and velvet, shaving with a borrowed razor and tying back hair that had by now become too long. Aurelle looked as perfect as always, picking out a dress of burgundy and pale cotton that seemed like a dark reflection of her hair. That, she wore in a caul today, while her hands were covered in gloves of red kid leather.

"We need to go find the library," Greave said when they were ready. "It has to be here."

"If it's just a matter of going to the square, we could wait a little longer," Aurelle said.

Greave shook his head. "There's no time to waste, not when Nerra is ..."

The worst part was that he didn't know what Nerra was now. With the scale sickness, she could be just as he had last seen her, or twisted into an inhuman form by now in a sudden change. She could be dead. No, Greave wouldn't think like that. He would be strong. He would solve this problem.

They set out for the city's main square, hope filling Greave with images of what it would be like. There would be a tower rising over all of it, precisely at the heart of the city. There would be scholars in dark robes going back and forth, debating the latest knowledge. There would be people looking on in awe ...

There wasn't any of that. What he saw instead made Greave want to shout in frustration.

A tower did indeed stand at the heart of the city's main square, but it was no taller than his waist. It was perfectly carved, even down to tiny windows of stained glass that sat in its dark stone walls. It stood in the middle of a circle of stone a dozen feet across, perhaps a little more. In that circle was a miniature representation of each of the buildings of the inner city, marked with their purpose. The sphere of the inn they had stayed in was there, as were the other towers. The central tower had "Library of Astare" on it, along with another legend below, in runes Greave recognized as belonging to the time of dragons. More symbols stood around the city, the words for knowledge in a dozen languages, spaced out by dividers that looked like the progress of the sun and moon.

He stood there, and he stared. Then he fell to his knees, tears falling from his eyes in a way he was sure they never would have from either of his brothers'.

Aurelle held him. "It's all right," she said. "It's just a cruel joke."

"It's not all right," Greave said. "I came here to save my sister, and now all I have to show for it is this." He swept a hand at it all, wishing that he could break it all apart. He walked away, his head in his hands, feeling tricked, feeling *broken.*

None of this made *sense.*

Unless that was the point. Greave stopped there, standing. He couldn't give up, when Nerra's life was on the line. He had to think.

He knew that there was a library. The books had been clear on that, and the House of Scholars alluded to it, even if they would not allow the unworthy entrance. If there were only this joke, it would be common knowledge by now. So this ... this had to be more. It had to be some kind of test.

"There's a trick to this," Greave said. "There has to be."

He tried to recall what he'd learned of old languages. The runes on the tower had to be the first step. He stared at them, trying to translate them.

"Greave, don't torment yourself," Aurelle said, clearly trying to protect him.

Greave knew there was something to it, though. "'All is made known in the fullest light of knowledge.'" It sounded like a motto of the House of Scholars, but Greave had not heard it. More than that, why would it be the fullest light? The poet in him insisted that didn't quite fit. He stared at the model again, at the dividers that spaced out the symbols for knowledge.

The answer eluded him, and he walked around the model, sure that there had to be an answer in there, but unable to see it. Light glinted from the model, making Greave blink, but also making him think about light, and its properties. Was it something to do with reflection, refraction, the different colors of light?

When was the fullest light?

Greave froze again as the possibility of an answer came to him. Could it be that? Truly?

Greave stood there, no longer pacing, just waiting now.

"What are you doing, Greave?" Aurelle asked. She wrapped her arms around him. "Come on, we should go."

"Trust me," Greave said. "Please, just trust me."

He continued to stand there as the sun rose, trying to judge the moment when it reached its zenith. There would be only seconds now.

"What are we waiting for?" Aurelle asked, standing by his side.

"For noon," Greave said.

Even as he said it, the sun reached the right angle, shining in through the windows that had been so cleverly cut into the model. There had to be some arrangement of mirrors to amplify things just so, and even then the effect was subtle enough that no one would have spotted it, or understood it, if they didn't know what they were looking for.

The symbol of the House of Scholars shone out in the bright colors of stained glass, striking a spot on the floor of the model city. It seemed to be in the middle of one of the open squares of houses, in one of the green spaces that filled it. There was a stone built arch there, perfect in miniature. Greave had no doubt about what would lie beyond it.

"You did it," Aurelle said, staring at Greave with surprise, but also respect. "You've found the library!"

Chapter Twenty Four

When the guards came to drag him to his execution, Renard knew it for what it was.

He'd seen the faces of men who wanted to kill him before, and this was like a cut down version of that, shorn of the anger, but still with the same twist of certainty to it, the same hardness that said that he wouldn't be able to change their minds with a well-placed word or a coin.

"Well, lads," he said, as they dragged him from his cell in manacles. "How has Lord Carrick decided to have me killed?"

They looked round at him in surprise, as if they thought he shouldn't have been able to work out what all this was about.

"You'll see," one of them assured him, as they made their way up from the featureless stone and straw of the dungeon.

"Ah, something bad, is it?" Renard asked. Then, without pausing, he elbowed the man in the ribs and ran as fast as his chains would allow him. It wasn't very fast, but it wasn't as though he had much to lose at this point, either.

Of course, the problem with trying to run while chained was that it simply didn't let a fellow move very fast. The same problem applied to trying to *fight* while chained too, although Renard did at least manage to get his chains around a guard's neck before one of them slammed the pommel of a knife into his skull, making him see as many stars as there were in all the heavens.

They pretty much carried him up the stairs after that, which seemed only fair to Renard. A man shouldn't have to walk to his own execution. They took him out into a courtyard, ringed by high walls that even he couldn't climb in chains. There were peasant folk there, crammed in tight and surrounded by guards to keep them in line. Yselle was there, and Renard had the feeling that having to watch this was part of the lesson that Lord Carrick wanted them to learn. He looked over to her, but did not dare declare what he felt while he did so. That would just have seen her hurt. There was a gallows set up, of course, and on it a burly executioner stood, next to a block, axe in hand.

Lord Carrick stood above it all on a balcony, looking on with apparent indifference as the guards carried Renard up the wood of the gallows' steps.

"Renard the thief," he said, as Renard reached the top. "You stand before me having stolen from me. You will pay for that."

"Beheading, my lord?" Renard shot back. "That's hardly very original."

"Eventually beheading," Lord Carrick replied. "First, my man shall cut away your fingers. Then your hands. Then your feet. He will continue, until you are in sufficiently small pieces for everyone who had gold from you to have a part of you. Then, if you still breathe, you will be beheaded."

"Ah," Renard said.

"Do you have anything left to say for yourself?" Lord Carrick asked. "Would you like to beg for clemency? People sometimes do."

"Does it do them any good?" Renard asked. Lord Carrick's expression told him the answer. "Then I would simply like to say that while there are many things in my life I suppose I should regret, robbing you blind was not one of them, my lord."

There, that sounded suitably pithy, and it did a good job of masking the raw terror running inside him too. He had to find a way of getting out of here, had to find a way clear.

Of course, he could have *been* clear by now if only he'd taken the Hidden up on their offer, but some things were worse even than being carved up like a side of beef. They could do things to a man that would make a horrific death seem pleasant by comparison.

Although Renard had to admit that it seemed more than bad enough right now.

An honorable man would have marched to the block. A hero would have set his hand down on it and dared the executioner to do his worst, giving the common folk something to remember this day, something to inspire them.

Since Renard was neither of those things, he fought the whole way, so that the guards had to tie him to the block with length after length of crude rope while he bit and elbowed and kneed. Eventually though, there wasn't enough movement left in him to fight longer. There was only the executioner standing over him with that axe.

"Begin," Lord Carrick commanded.

The executioner raised his axe. It seemed to happen impossibly slowly, and for a moment, Renard wondered if it was some trick of his mind, slowing down these last moments, giving him at least the illusion of time in which to act even if there was none.

After several seconds of it, though, he realized that the man really *was* moving that slowly. He ground to a halt, then his axe went clattering onto the floor as he froze in place, ringing out in a tumble of metal.

Three hooded figures stepped out from the crowd.

Renard could only watch as Void, Verdant, and Wrath stepped into place in front of Lord Carrick's balcony. The guards did not move to stop them, although they looked between them and Lord Carrick as if trying to decide who they feared more.

Verdant stepped over to the executioner. She touched him lightly on the lips, and he gasped, seeming to regain the ability to move all in a rush. He scrambled back from her like a mouse from a cat, even though he towered over her.

"What is the meaning of this?" Lord Carrick boomed down from his spot on the balcony.

"My lord," Void said, that blank mask of his staring up at Lord Carrick. "It is good to see you again, after so long. I trust that our arrangement worked out well for you?"

"Our arrangement…" Lord Carrick stood there staring down at him. For a moment, Renard thought that the man might actually be arrogant enough to try to deny it. "Yes, of course."

"And that you have not forgotten the boon you said you would owe us," Void continued.

In that moment, Renard knew what he was going to ask for. It seemed that Lord Carrick knew it too.

"No," he said, pointing an accusing finger at Renard. "This man is mine to kill. He has stolen from me!"

"And we have need of a thief," Verdant said in that too honeyed voice of hers.

Wrath joined in, cracking his knuckles. "Unless you want to break your word to us? Unless you want the Hidden for an enemy?"

"I..." Lord Carrick looked from them to Renard and back. Renard could feel the hatred there. He found himself hoping that hatred would be enough for him to order some guard to put a blade in him anyway. It would probably be better than what the Hidden had planned.

"Take him," Lord Carrick snapped, gesturing to Renard. "He is yours now, to do with as you wish. Take him and go."

Damn it, Renard couldn't even rely on a man like his lordship to do the stupid, cruel thing. He could only watch as Void and the others came over to him. The Hidden's leader nodded to Verdant, who touched the ropes that held Renard.

He smelled the scent of rot that went bone deep, and deeper, the scent of blooms opening in a deep forest somewhere, already consumed with fungi. Even as he smelled it, the hemp of the ropes seemed to blacken and fall from him, crawling with maggots.

Wrath lifted him to his feet easily. He took the chains that held Renard, and he snapped them.

"I've already told you that I'm happy here," Renard said to Void.

The other man's cloaked shoulders moved up and down in a shrug. "That does not matter. You have been given to us now, in law. If you try to run, we will hunt you. If you fight us, we will do things to you that will make children weep when their mothers tell them of it."

The worst part was that there was no drama in the way he said those words. They were as cold and even as a grave slab.

"You could have come with us before," Verdant said. "There would have been such rewards."

"And we would not have had to call in a promise made to us," Void said.

Renard tried to think of a good way out of this. There was none.

"If you try to fight, I will hurt you," Wrath said.

"And I will find the one you looked at so sweetly as they dragged you out," Verdant promised. "We'll hurt her too."

"You–"

Void held up a hand and the silence was like a club, stopping them all.

"Enough of this," he said. "We have what we came for. Renard the thief, you will come with us, as you were always going to come with us."

"You're claiming it is fate, now?" he asked.

The Hidden's leader made a papery sound. It took Renard a second to recognize it as a laugh.

"It is simply the will of the Hidden. We get what we want, thief. Now come; you have an item to procure for us."

Renard went. As he did, he glanced back to Lord Carrick, wondering if it was too late to ask him to execute him anyway. It would probably be a lot quicker than everything his new companions had planned for him.

Chapter Twenty Five

Vars was waiting when the army returned to Royalsport. He stood atop the castle's battlements, looking out in fear, knowing that when his father and his brother returned, he was going to face their full wrath for what he had done. For what he had failed to do.

No, I did all I could, he insisted to himself.

Lyril was not there. Vars was surprised by that. In recent weeks, she had been by his side almost constantly, yet now she was gone. He could guess why: the rumors about him coming back alone when he was supposed to be protecting his sister had already started.

When his father got back, he would be disinherited. Vars was sure of it. Below, the city bustled, smoke coming from the chimneys, the streams currently at low tide between Royalsport's many islands. Vars stood there until he could see the advance of the soldiers returning, the blocks of the troops moving in concert, the Knights of the Spur shining as they rode in gleaming cohorts. His fear built with every step they took closer, until Vars was sure that the best thing to do was flee, run from the castle and never come back.

He swallowed and headed down through the castle, hastening past servants who seemed to be hurriedly preparing for the return of the king, polishing floors and silver, brushing dust from tapestries and setting out food in readiness. He pushed one aside as he moved through a hall with low beams overhead, heading for his rooms.

In those, he grabbed a sack, trying to decide what he would need to take. He threw in clothes, obviously, then coins. He took silver candlesticks, reasoning that he would be able to sell them, and grabbed jewelry.

If he was not here, then his father and his brother could not do anything to him.

He was still trying to decide what to take when a servant appeared in the doorway.

"What?" Vars snapped, his fear turning into anger, as it so often did.

"Your highness," the servant said. "You need to come. Your father..."

Was this what it had come to? Had they sent servants to drag him there? Would there be knights waiting outside the door, ready to carry him away?

"One moment," Vars said, trying to think of a way out of it. Perhaps he could still slip away.

"Your highness," the servant said. "Your father has fallen in battle. You must come to the great hall."

Sheer shock dropped Vars to his knees. He tumbled, not understanding.

"My lord, can I help you?" the servant asked.

Vars waved the servant off, climbing back to his feet by grabbing onto a statue of some hero Vars didn't even know the name of. He didn't feel very heroic right then, barely had the strength to pull himself up again. The weight of the statue held Vars in place, staring at the servant there, barely comprehending the words.

"Say that again," he said. His voice was barely more than a whisper.

"Your father," the servant said. "He has fallen. Not dead, but he will not wake. And your brother Rodry is gone."

That took time to sink in past the wash of fear that had been filling Vars's mind. The meaning of it took even longer. Seconds passed in silence, emotions flaring through him one after the other, and all at once. Fear, horror... relief. It was too much, too overwhelming to consider.

His father was fallen in battle. Vars could just about comprehend that. But for Rodry to be gone too...

"I'm... I'm *king*?" Vars said.

"Yes, your highness," the servant said, and then corrected himself. "A regent, at least, while your father is... unwell."

Vars stood there, blinking, trying to wait for it to make sense. Then he pushed past the servant, all but running down in the direction of the great hall. He wound his way through the castle's corridors, down spiral stairs and along galleries filled with the faces of dead kings. Would his father's features be set there now? In time, would *his*?

Vars came to the great hall and had to shove his way inside, there were so many people there. There were nobles there, and knights, and more, the tables pushed back to the walls to make room for them, the normal demarcations of the carpets for each group forgotten in the crush. Vars had never been in a battle, but now he was starting to get a sense of what it might be like, and he was glad that he had avoided it.

"Step back!" he commanded. "Let me *through*."

To his surprise, people did. They gave way to him, letting him to the front where, upon the dais that held the thrones for king and queen, his father lay upon a table set with white cloth, still in his full armor.

For a moment, Vars was certain that the servant had been mistaken, and that he was dead, yet no, it was clear that he still breathed. Vars stood over him, looking down, knowing that if he had only protected his sister better, this would not have happened. He looked out over the crowd and found Lenore there, standing with Erin's support, their mother holding to them as she sobbed.

Vars stared out at the rest of them, seeing the eyes looking back, those of knight and noble alike. He knew what he had to do. Carefully, barely daring to do it, he moved back until he could seat himself on the throne.

"Take my father to his rooms," he said. "Send for Physicker Jarran and have him tend to him. Queen Aethe will no doubt wish to attend on him, and Princess Lenore must be tended to as well, after all she has suffered."

An honor guard of the Knights of the Spur came to carry his comatose father away. Servants led the queen and Lenore from the hall, too. To everyone watching, it must have seemed like an act of kindness, but Vars breathed a sigh of relief that all of those who might have challenged him in that moment were gone.

"Where are my brothers?" Vars asked. "Tell me what has happened."

Commander Harr stepped forward. Vars had always disliked the way the man's gaze seemed to see through him. "The news is dire, your highness. It seems that Prince Rodry died in the south. There has been no news of Prince Greave. Were he in Royalsport, I am sure he would be here."

Vars could barely believe the idea that Rodry might be dead. He was too strong for that, too impossible to beat. Vars had been sure that no man alive could kill him. Now, just like that, he was gone.

"And the battle?" Vars said. "We beat them?"

The commander nodded. "With the bridge down, there is no more access for the southern armies."

"It's not that simple," a voice called from the side. To Vars's surprise, it was Erin who stepped forward, dressed in armor as if she'd been away playing at fighting. There was a man beside her who might have been a monk, save for the sword sheathed at his back.

"I'm sure the commander knows war better than you, sister," Vars said.

"But he doesn't know what my friend here knows," Erin said, gesturing to the monk.

"And who are *you*?" Vars demanded of the man. He looked ragged, bloody, wounded. Hardly a man to listen to at all.

"My name ... I've had several," the man said. "I was known as Brother Odd for a while, of the Isle of Leveros. Before that, I was ... Sir Oderick the Mad."

Around him, the room erupted at the name. Vars could understand why. He'd heard the stories of Sir Oderick, of the slaughters, the chaos he caused. Around him, he could hear the men murmuring in fear.

"... has he returned?"

"... should have his head ..."

He didn't want to risk angering a man like that, though.

"What news do you have, Sir Oderick?" Vars asked.

"Leveros has fallen," the other man said. "King Ravin has breached its neutrality, and is bringing his armies in from the east."

Again, the room exploded in noise, everyone there seeming to have a demand, or a plan, or a worried exclamation all at once. Some seemed to be terrified that all their forces were to the kingdom's south now, having been sent to the bridge. Others were disbelieving, or demanding to know what Vars would do ...

It was too much. So many demands all at once were too much to think through. Perhaps his father or his brother might have stood up and shouted for silence, but Vars was terrified that no one would listen. Instead…

…instead, he did the only thing he could think of, and ran from the hall, back to an antechamber, leaning against the wall until he thought that he could breathe again.

No one followed. It helped that there were guards outside the room, but even so, he had expected the press of courtiers to be overwhelming. Vars stood there among the tapestries depicting heroes, among the finery that his house had won through strength, and he felt like a fraud.

When his half-sister's husband-to-be walked into the room, he felt even worse. He felt sure that Finnal would have talked to Lenore and learned what Vars had done, that he would be angry. Instead, he moved over to a low marquetry table and poured himself a glass of wine from a decanter.

"Would you like one, your majesty?" Finnal asked, and offered Vars the glass. Vars took it and downed it smoothly. He had to remember that he had seen the other side of Finnal in the House of Sighs too, that he was more than just the pleasant young man his sister doted on.

"Why are you here?" Vars asked.

"To assure you of my family's loyalty to our new king regent," Finnal said. "My father would do it, but he has been called away to our estates."

Vars paused for a moment, trying to make sense of it. What exactly was Finnal saying?

Finnal sighed. "King Vars, the truth is that you will need friends at a time like this. The kingdom has taken a great blow, and faces great dangers. Clearly you are the man to lead, but we must all rally around you. Especially when there are… questions about why you were not at the battle."

"I…" Vars tried to think of something to say. Normally he was good at making up lies and excuses, but this was all too much.

"No doubt you were led in the wrong direction by Quiet Men," Finnal said, "who knew that had you been there to protect Princess Lenore, you would have slaughtered them."

"Yes," Vars lied. "That's it exactly."

"Then this truth must be made known," Finnal said. "For we both know how quickly vile rumors can spread. Thankfully, you have a friend in me, Vars. I will see to it that the right people hear you were a hero in this."

"And why would you do that?" Vars asked.

Finnal smiled. "Because we're about to be family. You *are* going to honor my upcoming marriage to Lenore, aren't you? On the terms your father agreed to?"

"I…" Vars was about to protest that this wasn't the moment to be thinking about a marriage, but the truth was that he needed the allies. Besides, what did Vars care who his half-sister was given to in marriage, or when? "Yes, of course."

"And we'll be married as quickly as possible?" Finnal said. "There is no sense in delaying. The kingdom needs this joining."

"Yes," Vars said. "Yes, you're right."

"That's wonderful," Finnal said, putting an arm around his shoulders. "I'm sure that we will be such *good* friends."

Chapter Twenty Six

Lenore lay in bed, unable to rest, the world around her seeming bleak and empty and dark. She tried closing her eyes, but each time she did that, it felt as though the Quiet Men were waiting for her, ready to kidnap her again, and kill those around her. They were dead, or stranded across the other side of the Slate, but that made no difference, not to this.

Her rooms were as beautiful as they had ever been, gilded and painted, every corner decorated with flowers or with embroidery, in a space that any princess should have loved. Yet now, they felt as much a prison as the room at the inn had, because Lenore didn't dare go out to face the rest of the court.

Even thinking about the inn made her shudder. She couldn't think about it; she wouldn't. What else did that leave to think about, though? Was she supposed to stare at the absences where her maidservants had been, thinking about all the things that had been done to them before they'd either been murdered or sent out in a cruel kind of message to the world? Was she supposed to think about Rodry, standing there in his last moments, dying so that Lenore could escape? Or was she supposed to think about her father, lying comatose in his rooms, unmoving while her mother and the physicker stood over him?

Any one of those things would have been enough to make Lenore break down in tears before. Now, the combination of them felt like enough to push her into a space beyond tears, where the pain turned into something else, and she could do nothing but lie there, staring at the walls.

She was still staring when Finnal entered the room. He looked as splendid as ever, the golden counterpart to her, fair-skinned and handsome, graceful as a dancer in every movement. He wore a silver-worked doublet and hose, but he outshone any costume he could wear.

"You came," Lenore said, sitting up, grateful beyond words that he was there. Finnal's presence would make everything better. He would hold her and chase away the nightmares that kept her from sleep, he would—

"Be quiet," Finnal said, in a surprisingly cold voice. "Your role in this conversation is to listen, not to prattle as you have spent every other conversation prattling."

"But Finnal—" Lenore began, and the look in his eyes held such contempt that she froze, unable to speak.

"While your father was around, I had to play the part of the loving suitor," Finnal said. "I had to be your perfect prince, and for what? A girl whose value is now *greatly* diminished?"

Lenore didn't know how to react to that. "I…I am a princess of this realm!"

"One who has been captured and abused by the south," Finnal said. "Frankly, I'm astonished that *my* father wants us to continue with getting married. Still, at least the link to your title is a useful one."

"What's wrong?" Lenore asked, not able to believe what she was hearing. "Why are you doing this?"

"Why am I saying what I think rather than simpering along like a courtier?" Finnal shot back. "Because your brother Vars is a much more practical man than your father. He will see you married to me without any foolish notions of love being involved."

"But I thought—"

"You thought that because you were a princess, anyone they brought to you had to fall in love with you?" Finnal said. He laughed. "Stupid girl. I've spent more time in the House of Sighs since we met than with you."

The rumors…Lenore had dismissed them, but now, she could see that it was all true.

"Do you…do you even like me?" Lenore asked.

"Enough to sire an heir," Finnal said. "Enough to enjoy you, obviously. But there will be rules to our marriage. Let us be clear that your role is to provide a connection to royal blood, and that is it. You will provide me with heirs, and your presence will make me royal enough that people will listen. Beyond that, I will seek my enjoyment… elsewhere, and you will remember your place. You will be spending most of your time in our new estates, away from the world. You will not disobey me on any matter, or contradict my word. Do you understand?"

"And what happens if I refuse?" Lenore asked.

Finnal gave her a baleful look. "Your brother will give you to me in marriage regardless. Once I am your husband, I will be free to do with you as I wish. It would not be wise to anger me."

Lenore felt a knot of fear building inside her. She had thought that she had suffered the worst the world had to offer. Now, it seemed that Finnal was worse still. He turned on his heel as if it didn't matter what impact he'd just had on her, what damage he'd done, then left without another word.

⚜ ⚜ ⚜

Lenore wasn't sure how much longer she lay there. She didn't want to look at anyone, didn't want to do anything, didn't want to rise. She ignored food when one of the servants offered it, lay dry-eyed, wishing that she could find even tears in all this.

She was still lying there when the door opened, and a figure she had never thought to see walked in.

"Orianne?" she said.

Her former maidservant stood there, tall and elegant, her dark hair tied back. Her gown was simple now by noble standards, pale linen and lace rather than silk and velvet. She didn't pause, but rushed over to Lenore's side, hugging her tightly.

Lenore wept then, as she hadn't been able to before. She wept all the tears that had been held back, for her brother, her father, her maids, herself. Orianne held onto her quietly, just there for her, until it seemed she had wept so much that she could have filled the Slate with her tears.

"How are you here?" Lenore asked. "I sent you away. I told the guards not to let you in."

"None of that matters," Orianne said. "I heard what happened to you, and a few guards weren't going to keep me out."

"But *how*?" Lenore asked.

Orianne shrugged. "Meredith at the House of Sighs called in some favors with those guards who had visited. I hope you don't mind."

Lenore thought about the way she'd reacted the time the House of Sighs' mistress had been there. She winced at the thought.

"I... I was so horrible to you," Lenore said. "I made you leave because you'd said the wrong thing about Finnal, but you were right about him all along."

"I know," Orianne said.

"He came to me a little while ago," Lenore said. "He told me that our marriage would be a sham, that we would be married in name only, and that I would be shut away in comfort while he dealt with everything that mattered. How could I not see what he was?"

"You couldn't see, because you were in love," Orianne said. "Do you think I can't forgive that?"

"I don't know," Lenore said. "Can you?" She thought for only another second before she said the next part, and she only thought about it because it seemed impossible that Orianne might accept. "Would you... would you consider coming back and being my maid again?"

She'd lost so much in the previous days that it seemed impossible to her that there could be any goodness coming out of it all like this.

"Of course," Orianne said.

"Thank you," Lenore said, hugging her again.

Orianne started to pull her to her feet.

"What are you doing?" Lenore asked.

"We're going to get you up and make you look like a princess again," Orianne said.

"That won't... it won't change anything."

"No," Orianne agreed, "it won't. It won't take away any of the hurt, or bring back the lost. But it will change the way people look at you."

She picked out a mourning dress of dark velvet, laying it out for Lenore, then helping her into it. She brushed Lenore's hair, helping her with her makeup and her jewels, until she stood in front of the mirror, and no trace of all the turmoil she felt inside shone through.

"You are strong," Orianne said, "and we will show that to this would-be husband of yours."

"He *will* be my husband," Lenore said. "Vars is ruling in Father's place, and he will give me away. It probably even suits him, having me where I can't talk about him not being there for me."

"Then you will be married," Orianne said. "But there are always ways to change things, and to fight back. You will have my help at every step."

"Thank you," Lenore said.

"You can thank me by being the princess we all know you can be. For now though, how about we go for a walk around the castle walls? It will be good for you to be in the sunlight, and to be seen."

Lenore wasn't sure if she could do it, after all that had happened. Even so, Orianne's presence seemed to lend her strength. She would do this, all of this, no matter where it led.

Chapter Twenty Seven

Devin stood over the forge, channeling magic, focusing. So many times now, that magic had flared and burst out, caught only by the wards that Master Grey had put in place. He had felt so close each time he tried to work with the star metal, yet each time he reached for the traces of the magic that sat within him, it seemed to slip and twist, too powerful to rein in.

"This time," Devin said, breathing the words aloud to the steel, to the world, turning them into a kind of prayer, a chant. "This time."

He focused himself, feeling the magic within, heating the forge. He pushed that magic into the star metal as he heated it, making it glow first red, then gold, then white. Devin took it from the forge, striking it as it cooled, each blow of the hammer against the anvil sending flares of power through it.

He was doing this, he was actually *doing* it!

Before, he had tried to force the metal to do what he wanted, but it didn't work like that. He had to coax it and guide it, letting it flow into position under the weight of the magic. Devin kept going, kept working. He lifted the blade, quenched it, sharpened it. For a guard, he used a piece of what looked like bone, sitting on the bench, already cut for that purpose. He wrapped the grip in strips of leather, and set in place a pommel that held glass that looked like an eye staring out at the world.

By the time he was done, Devin was sweating, and not just from the heat of the forge. He could feel the effort the magic had taken now, leaving him weak. He stood there staring at the finished sword, the blade blue-black where most would have shone, the balance elegant. Devin cut it through the air, feeling the thrum of something more than muscle behind the blow.

He looked around, wishing that Master Grey were here to see this moment. Master Grey had not shown his face here again, though, had not been there to answer any of the many questions Devin had for him now. He was off about some unfathomable errand of his own.

Devin set down his tools, hearing the ring of steel against their brackets. He shut the forge down, setting the sword in place on a stand, wanting nothing more than air now that he had completed his task.

He ascended the stair from the cavernous depths of the forge, wondering if he might find a way to visit Lenore. It seemed impossible, though, that the castle guards would simply allow some peasant smith to visit the princess in her rooms, whatever connection he claimed to her brother.

Her brother. Devin's heart tightened at the thought that Rodry was lost. The news was all around the castle, and he didn't know how to respond to it. The thought of everything that had happened…why had Master Grey insisted that Devin stay behind when he could have helped?

Devin came up out of the castle's depths, blinking in the sunlight, trying to get a sense of how long he'd been down there this time, working with a metal that seemed not to respond the way iron or steel might have, that needed magic even to soften it. He looked around at the open square of the courtyard. It seemed so much fuller than it had before, horses hobbled there since there wasn't enough room in the stables for all of them, soldiers moving back and forth as they carried messages or ran errands. There were courtiers here and there, standing out in the finery of their clothes.

The whole castle felt as though it was caught between states, no one quite knowing what was going on. Where before, everyone had seemed to move around the castle with purpose, about a hundred different tasks that made the place as a whole function, now there were servants standing as if waiting for commands, and soldiers sitting idle, practicing with blades or playing dice.

Devin stretched out his aching muscles, looked up toward the sky to guess at the weather, and his gaze fell on the battlements. There, walking out along them, Devin saw her: Lenore, accompanied by only a single maid!

He looked around for a way to get up there, saw stone steps, and hurried up them. From the top of the wall, he could see out over Royalsport, see the presence of extra soldiers down below, encamped around the castle now that they had returned. On another day, he might have stopped and breathed in the air there, looked down at the hustle and bustle of the city. Instead, he had eyes only for Lenore.

He rushed forward along the battlements, dodging past a guard making the rounds of them. Lenore was just ahead, staring out over the city, her sadness palpable even from here.

"Lenore!" Devin called out.

Her handmaid was turning toward him, moving to block the way.

"Her highness wishes to be alone," she said, raising a hand to stop him.

"No, it's all right Orianne," the princess said. In amongst the sadness that seemed to fill her features, Devin thought that he caught the briefest flash of a smile. Her handmaid stepped back to let Devin pass, but she still gave him a look suggesting that Devin had best not do anything to harm the princess.

Devin moved closer to Lenore. She looked tired, as beautiful as ever, but as if everything she had suffered had drained something out of her, leaving her hollow, empty.

"Devin," Lenore said, managing a faint smile. "It's good to see you."

"I'm glad you're safe," Devin said. "I... I heard about Rodry."

Lenore bit her lip, tears springing to her eyes.

"I'm sorry," Devin said. "I didn't mean to upset you. It was just... he was good to me."

"He was like that," Lenore said, leaning back against the battlements. "He was always so generous. If you were his friend, you were his friend for life. And he was brave, too. I wish he'd been a little less brave. Maybe he'd still be alive."

"I think, to get you back, he'd do it all over again," Devin said. "And if he didn't..."

He stopped himself before he said that he would. There were things he probably wasn't supposed to say to a princess. Devin wasn't sure what all of them were, though, and that just made the whole thing more complicated.

"I know," Lenore said. "Would you... would you sit with me a while? It seems like people have been avoiding me since I got back."

Devin nodded. "If I'd thought they would let me through, I would have come to your rooms. I'm glad I spotted you out here."

"I'm glad too," Lenore said.

They sat together on the edge of the battlements. From here, it was possible to see the whole of the city, and some of the lands beyond, the fields stretching out in gold and green, out toward the forests in the distance.

They sat there, and for the first minute or two, they *just* sat. Devin wasn't sure what to say. He wasn't sure what someone like him could have to say to a princess, or what to say to Lenore after everything she'd lost. It felt as if all he could do was be there.

"I'm sorry," he said after a minute. "I'm not very good at this."

"You seem to be doing fine so far," Lenore said. "Most of the people so far have either told me how sorry they are, or gone on with making plans for my wedding. My mother is grieving over my father, Vars is ... Vars, Greave is missing. It's not a time when my family is exactly going to gather around me."

"If there's anything you need," Devin said, "just say it, and I'll do it."

Lenore looked surprised by that, and it occurred to Devin that there probably were many things that *he* could do for *her.*

"Thank you," she said. "I think most of the people around here are mostly thinking about what I can still do for them." She paused for a second or two. "My husband-to-be definitely is."

"Is everything ..." Devin stopped himself. "Sorry, I was about to ask if everything was all right."

Lenore smiled wanly. "Almost nothing is. You wanted to do something for me? Tell me about how things are going for you. Tell me about something normal."

"I'm not sure that there's much that's normal about it," Devin said. "I have been spending every day in a forge in the cellar, trying to get metal that refuses to respond to anything but magic to turn into a sword, and I've ... I've finished it, only to just realize that it was going to be either your father or your brother I was due to give it to."

"Does that mean you're going to go?" Lenore asked.

Devin shook his head. "I don't know. I've finished, but I don't think Master Grey is finished with me. As for leaving ... I don't want to do that."

"I wouldn't want you to either," Lenore said. "The metal you're working with responds to magic? So Master Grey is helping you?"

"He ..." Devin wasn't sure what to say, how much to reveal even with someone like Lenore. "There are spells woven all through the forge. He isn't there anymore though. I'm not sure where he's gone."

"Who knows where sorcerers go?" Lenore said. "When we were children, we would have lessons with him sometimes, and it always felt as though, for every one thing he told us, there were another dozen that he didn't."

Devin nodded at that, thinking of everything that he'd found in Master Grey's rooms, the things that he'd found in the man's journal. Was any of it true? Was he really the one who had the potential to change the world?

Right then, he realized that, for a minute or two, none of it mattered. It was enough that he was here with the princess, enough that, for a few moments, everything seemed to be at peace. They sat there with one another while below, the castle continued to whirl and bustle, and even though they didn't say anything, it was enough.

"We need to go, your highness," Orianne said after a while.

Lenore sighed and rose. "I know." She turned to Devin. "I have enjoyed this."

"Me too," Devin said.

"Are you serious about me being able to ask you for anything in the coming days?"

Devin nodded. He knew it was an easy thing to say, but he meant it. And in that moment, he knew what he had to do with the sword. Rodry had intended the sword as a wedding present, so he would see it given to Lenore. It was the least he could do for his former friend.

Chapter Twenty Eight

King Ravin stood on the deck of his flagship, sunlight shining from his armor, and knew that the world was his to take. It was the feeling that he woke with each morning, and the one that he lay down with each night: the certainty that he was not as other men were, that he, of all of them, was the one able to reach out and have what he wished from the world.

Around him, his soldiers stood in careful ranks, nestled at the heart of a fleet of galleys and cogs, the flagship large and broad sailed, dark wood painted with red shapes that might have been intended to signify the blood of his foes or the fire of a world torn down. He'd had it built, as he'd had all the rest of it built.

"How long until the island will come into sight?" Ravin demanded of the closest sailor.

The man fell to his knees, head bowed. "An hour or less, Majesty."

It was a wonder to Ravin that his men could chart these things so precisely. Not because the skills seemed impossible, but because his men had learned them so quickly and so well. He had built a body of sailors willing to go beyond the sight of land, just as he had built all the rest of it.

He had planned for this, planned for all of it, almost since the moment when he had taken the throne.

He could still hear the whisper of his father's last breath, caught in surprise, a dagger plunging into him that was so thin it barely left a mark. Another dozen daggers had risen and fallen that night, killing the others his father had sired, and their mothers, and those who might support them.

Ravin turned to the sailor. "Do you know what the most powerful weapon for a king is?"

The man looked shocked that his king would ask such a question. "No, Majesty."

"It is the ability to plan more than his enemies, to know more than them, to set things in motion knowing how they will turn out."

The sailor stared, but then, such men probably had little experience talking to their betters. King Ravin didn't mind; it was still better than talking to the courtiers who prattled round him, promising this or that, flattering and scheming.

"I have been planning this since ... well, since before I became king," Ravin said. "Becoming king was only a part of it, and that took enough planning. It is not enough to kill those who stand in your way, of course. One must arrange things to have control afterwards, forge alliances, or at least the appearance of alliances."

Ravin drew the man to his feet. He looked up into the tangle of lines and sails above. Men clambered among it, swaying with the rest of the ship as it rolled from side to side. "Consider the ... rigging, I believe it is called?"

"Yes, Majesty?" the man said.

"Such a complex web of ropes, each with a purpose, each moving in a specific way. If they tangle wrong, the progress of the ship is impeded. Disaster might follow."

"Yes, Majesty," the sailor agreed, although Ravin could see that he didn't understand the point.

"Now imagine that it was a thousand times more complex, and that any slip among it would result in disaster, not just for a single ship, but for an entire nation," Ravin said. "*That* has been my life. Do you know that I was not initially meant to be a king? That I was least among my father's children, destined for little more than death when another ascended?"

The sailor nodded. "I ... have heard the stories, Majesty."

Ravin laughed. "Stories. I had the stories *written*. A king must look a certain way, be a certain way, and I took care to be all of it. I found which friends to make, and which to offer the appearance of friendship for as long as they could be useful. I learned when to be generous, and when to be cruel. I became king."

The sailor had settled into step beside him now, close as a confidant on a tour of a garden, except that they were walking the deck of a ship, among an armada of them, the promise of their foes' land somewhere in the distance.

"From the moment I became king, I knew that it was not enough," Ravin said. "My father thought it was, was content with his hunting and his gaming and his drinking. Oh, I affected to enjoy these things, of course; a king must appear as people expect, but I knew that people need more: they need purpose."

"Purpose, Majesty?" the sailor asked.

"Without it, they fall into bickering, into conflict, although they do that well enough anyway," King Ravin said with a laugh. "But give them a common goal, and they will work together. In this case, to reunite the kingdom that once was, north and south together. I have known that it was *my* purpose for almost as long as I have known that I was destined to be king."

"As you say, Majesty," the sailor said. It was as close to a disagreement as men dared around him.

"You don't agree? Speak freely."

"Just that you speak of all of this as if it is set by fate."

"It is set by my *will*," King Ravin said. "And by the care that I have taken. Can you imagine what it took to build up my Quiet Men and send them across the river over years? To create a navy in a kingdom that has never known the need? To lure my foes' forces south by daring to take their princess in the one time she would be vulnerable?"

"I cannot, Majesty," the sailor admitted.

"Of course you cannot," King Ravin said, but it was not cruel. It was simply the way that things were. "Just as I am sure that there are things of the sea that you must know, and I have never heard."

"Your Majesty is too kind," the sailor said.

"I have rarely been accused of that," King Ravin said. "You became a sailor when you were young, didn't you?"

The sailor looked at him in surprise that he might know that. Ravin always found it amusing that small people would think that he wouldn't know more than them.

"Your parents were killed as my army moved to put down rebels. They were not traitors, but they were there, and violent men strike as they wish." Ravin watched the man's eyes, saw the shock there, and the anger rising underneath it. "That is why, a year ago, you contacted certain people within my capital city. You believe them to be rebels. In fact, they are the puppets of a certain nobleman who even now resides in my dungeons."

The sailor started to move away, taking a hesitant step back.

"It is why you have a knife in the small of your back, ready to reach for," the king said. He looked levelly at the sailor. "Well, what are you waiting for, Togan Marr? I thought you said that you were prepared to die to rid the world of me?"

The sailor hesitated again, and King Ravin was bored with him now, so he nodded to two of the soldiers there. They grabbed the sailor, exactly as Ravin had ordered them to an hour ago. They lifted him, and with a lack of ceremony, flung him over the side of the ship, to be consumed by the waters below.

Ravin stood at the prow, now, waiting as the fleet grew close to the Isle of Leveros. It was beautiful in its way, the monastery spreading out over it rich with weathering and the patina of age. The fleet came close, not stopping, but slowing a little so that the boats that had taken the island for him could come out with supplies, reports, news. Flickers of light came, reflected from mirrors, in codes Ravin had devised himself for the purpose. Even so, he waited for a servant to approach, bowing low before he gave the king the news.

"The island is secure, my king," the man said.

"I know that," King Ravin said. "And with the island taken, the way is clear. What else?"

"News from the mainland," the man said. "Our people brought messages across. The enemy's forces have taken the bait and headed south."

Ravin waited in silence for the man to tell him something else, something *useful.*

"Prince Rodry is dead," the man said. "As is King Godwin."

"You're certain?"

"The prince crossed the bridge and succeeded in rescuing his sister, but was slain. King Godwin fell in battle at the bridge."

King Ravin allowed himself a smile. All was going as planned.

He continued to stand there, watching as the fleet around him progressed toward the Northern Kingdom. He stood there watching, planning, working out every one of the steps to follow as clearly as he might have done when crouched over a gaming board.

It was nearly sundown when he saw it in the distance: a thin sliver of land appearing on the horizon. It grew, the land of the Northern Kingdom becoming closer by the second. King Ravin stared at it hungrily.

Soon, it would be his.

Chapter Twenty Nine

Renard stood partway up a volcano, in front of a sheer rock wall that had to be fifty feet high, surrounded by the masked forms of the Hidden. Ahead lay the wall, and somewhere beyond that, an item that was both valuable and dangerous enough to draw him into all of this. He suspected that a more self-aware man might have seen that as some kind of metaphor for his life, but Renard had always made a point of dodging self-awareness the way he dodged watchmen's arrows.

The volcano itself was probably only a small one as such things went, but even so, it towered over Renard, stabbing up into the sky like a broken dagger thrust at the heavens. Around him, there were pools that steamed with water that stayed hot with the place's heat, while thin slivers of burning orange high above said that this was not the sleeping giant that he might have wished for.

"The mausoleum sits above," Void said. "There were stairs once, but now a man must climb to the entrance. Within, there will be defenses to prevent grave robbers."

"And I'm to get past them and get to the item you want," Renard said.

"Yes," Void said. He passed Renard a bag. "Your tools."

"Thank you. Just one question."

"No questions!" Wrath snapped from the side.

"This is kind of an important one: what does the item actually *look* like?"

"We believe it to be an amulet," Void said, while Wrath looked at him with undisguised hate. "Worked with dragon designs, no bigger than a man's hand."

Renard nodded. "And what about—"

"You are trying to delay," Verdant said from his other side. "Delaying will not work, nor pleading, nor anything else. Begin your work, thief, or I will fill your flesh with vines that expand through it."

Renard had no doubt that she could. He swallowed. "All right."

Renard focused his attention on the wall before him. It was vertical, but craggy and gnarled. Aside from the spots that looked glassy and sharp, the climb did not look difficult. Wrapping his hands in lengths of cloth to limit the potential for damage, Renard threw himself at the cliff and set off upward.

He'd climbed many things over the years: trees, walls, once an ornamental trellis when an angry husband had returned unexpectedly. This rock face was one of the easier ones, and Renard scampered up it almost as quickly as walking it.

Above, he found an entrance that made him stop: three blocks of carved stone formed a doorway, while the door itself was made from slabs of granite, carved with two dragons standing sternly. There was a lock set into it, and Renard fished out his picks. He was about to set to work when he spotted the second hole next to the obvious lock, one of the dragons' claws giving way to reveal it. In the main lock, Renard saw the point of a dart gleaming. He set to work on the hidden lock instead, and soon the door snapped open.

Within was a tunnel, set on each side with niches that held stone caskets. Each was carved in a language Renard didn't know, but it was thick with cobwebs. Renard took out a small lantern, lighting it so he could see his way as he went deeper.

The second trap almost caught him, buried as it was under layers of dust. Ordinarily, Renard would have spotted the shift in the floor from cobbles to black-and-white tiles, and would have been instantly suspicious. Now, his foot touched one before his mind registered the shift, and he threw himself back on instinct as a pendulum like blade scythed down from the ceiling, right through the spot where he had stood. He lay on his back panting, before forcing himself back to his feet.

He ignored the swish of the blades, ignored the floor that had triggered the trap. Access was the key. People who set traps like this wanted to be able to come and go if they needed to, which meant that there always had to be some way to disarm what they had put in place. He looked closely at the surrounding walls, examining each in turn, searching until he found a lever. Renard didn't pull it, but kept looking until he found the lock beside that lever, the sphere that would drop otherwise to release poison, or fire, or acid.

He disarmed it and set off, deeper into the complex. He came out into a large, open space, filled on every side with mausoleums and tributes to the dead. There was no roof in this space; it seemed to have been lost in some long ago eruption, or perhaps there had never been one. Perhaps this had always been a place where the sun could shine down on a floor patterned with a map that was not the world as Renard knew it. There was no Slate in that map, while Sarras to the west looked green and wholesome, alive, not devastated by fire.

There was another doorway at the far side of the room, this one outlined in what looked like gold rather than stone, with strange gouges on it, as if something had tried to get in there. Somehow, Renard knew that what he sought would be there. He set out across the floor...

A roar from above him made him look up in a terror that was so old it seemed to be baked into his bones. A shape sat above him, perched on the lip of the open space, and even though Renard had never seen a creature like the one that sat there, stories and pictures and more all told him what it was: a dragon.

How could there be a dragon? There had been no dragons seen in the kingdom in years. Terror flooded through Renard, and he forced himself to stare at it solely because he wasn't a man who gave in to terror... well, not often. He swallowed and stared up at it.

It was huge, and it was terrifying, blue scales gleaming, other colors seeming to flicker across them like a rainbow after a storm. Then the great mouth opened, and Renard realized just in time what was about to happen.

He flung himself down among the tombs as flames licked over his head, rolling between two, keeping low as he darted past another. He saw a blue form plunging down toward him, and he went flat again, great claws missing him by inches.

He was down there when he saw the bones and the corpses laid in one spot on the floor, a clear space among them just large enough for that huge form to curl up in sleep. Its nesting site! Why would a dragon nest *here* of all places?

The dragon landed, stalking through the tombs. Its jaws snapped out, taking the remains of a charred cow, obviously hunted on some farmer's lands. It gulped them down, then tossed them aside, and Renard took a moment to move sideways, away from the creature's path.

To his astonishment, it went to the door, clawing at the frame as if trying to fit through. It couldn't, too large by far to fit through there. That meant that soon, it would turn its attention back to Renard, and it would find him. Even if he weren't ripe from riding too long, it would scent him, and find him.

He needed a distraction. Crawling among the tombs, Renard searched until his hand found a discarded bone. He threw it, and the clatter of it among the stone of the rest seemed to be enough. The dragon's head snapped round, and its bulk shifted as it turned, following the sound, led by its hunger.

Renard moved in silence, hurrying down between the tombs, keeping his head low and scurrying for that doorway. He was a big man, but now he made himself small, knowing that one glimpse, one sound, might send a dragon's fire burning after him.

Renard felt the pebble beneath his foot, felt it give and scatter. It bounced from the nearest of the tombs, making a faint clunk as it did so.

Renard was already sprinting when the fire came behind him. He dove through the doorway, ahead of a spurt of flame, and there were golden doors there, open and hanging back against the wall. Renard slammed them, hearing the click of yet another lock. It didn't matter; he wasn't getting out that way. He heard the dragon's claws scrape against the door, but it held.

Renard breathed a sigh of relief, and dared to look around the room. It was smaller than the one beyond, but it seemed that every surface was gilded, or painted, or both. Scene after scene showed dragons, intertwining, fighting, flying. Where there must have been a hundred tombs in the room beyond, here, there was only one, standing at the center of the room, the figure of a man in full armor worked into its surface with its hands clasped over its chest.

Those hands held something, and instantly, Renard knew that it was what the Hidden had sent him to find. It was an octagonal amulet, small enough that it could have fit into the palm of his hand, if only barely. There were runes around the edges, each one filled in with a different color of gemstone. The amulet's heart was a single scale, and Renard could guess from the scratching on the door what kind of animal it had come from.

He reached for the amulet, and stopped, but there seemed to be no traps here, no tricks or threats. There was only the amulet, to take if he wished.

Renard lifted it, and the moment he did, he felt two things at once. The first was almost overwhelming. He felt the dragon outside the room, felt a connection to it that he could have reached out and touched easily. He felt... inexplicably, he knew that it was young, grown impossibly quickly on the magic of the world, filled with power. A name came into his head: *Alith.* More threads of connection reached out, stretching into the far distance. Renard could see now why the Hidden had wanted this: with something like this, they could reach out to a dragon, control it, use it.

That thought was almost enough to make him drop it, and not just because the knowledge of it seemed to fall into his head almost like a stone falling into a pool. Renard was a man who was used to flickers of memory coming out of nowhere, but that usually had to do with remembering the day after too much drink. This... the sheer enormity of what it represented was too much, the things a man might do too great.

He could also feel why they had sent him, rather than coming for it themselves; from the moment he touched it, something seemed to leach into him, pulling at all that made Renard who he was. Again, the knowledge was simply *there.* Wear this amulet or hold it for more than the briefest time, and someone would find their life force drawn from them.

He threw it from him, but it made no difference. It seemed that the pull of energy into the amulet merely slowed, rather than stopping. It was no more than a trickle, but left long enough, even a trickle would prove deadly.

The only question was what to do now. By rights, he should find another way out of this mausoleum, descend the volcano, and hand the amulet to the Hidden. Feeling it now though, feeling the power within it, Renard knew that he couldn't do that.

Keeping this amulet would kill him.

Yet he knew, then and there, even though the hordes of the world come after him, he would not give it back.

It was his now. His greatest theft of all time.

All he had to do was escape.

Chapter Thirty

"I'm not sure I can do this," Lenore said to her mother, as Queen Aethe adjusted the veil on her bridal gown. They stood in an antechamber outside the great hall, where her maidservants had set everything out for her before the queen had ordered them to leave.

"There, there," her mother said. "It is no more than nerves, and Finnal has insisted to Vars that things should go ahead as quickly as possible. Remember how you felt when you first set eyes on Finnal? That same joy will soon come to you again. This has been a… hard time, for all of us."

Did she think that Lenore didn't know that, when she'd been the one kidnapped by King Ravin's people? Did she think that Lenore was unaffected by the death of her brother, or her father? Her mother might be the one who knelt by the king's recumbent form for hours each day, but that didn't mean that Lenore hurt any less than her.

"Mother…" Lenore began, but Vars was there then, standing waiting in the spot her father should have held. He was dressed in royal robes of ermine and velvet, no crown on his head for now, but royal looking in every other respect.

"It's time," he said. He held out an arm for Lenore to take. "Your husband is waiting for you."

Lenore wanted to shy away, wanted to tell him that this was all some big mistake, but there was no give in his expression, no hint that he would even listen if she said something. Rodry would have listened, or one of her sisters, or even probably Greave, if they could get his head out of a book for long enough. Not Vars though.

"It's a pity that Greave can't be here," Lenore said, hoping for some delay, some postponement to what was to come.

Vars continued to hold his arm out, waiting. Lenore took the hint and rested her own gloved fingers lightly on his sleeve.

"If we were to wait for our brother to dig his head out of whatever book it's buried in, we might still be here a year from now," he said. "No, this wedding happens today. It will ... remind the people that there is still joy to be found even in times of great sadness."

The hesitation told Lenore that it wasn't the real reason he was going ahead with it. Probably that had to do with the alliance between the royal house and that of Duke Viris. The firmness of Vars's voice brooked no argument, though. Lenore had to do this.

Vars led her through into the great hall, and a fanfare pierced the air the moment they stepped inside.

This was not the packed, immensely decorated hall that it had been before, though. It was not filled with peasants free to come and go as they chose. It was not filled with joyous feasting, or even with many people.

There were a few nobles, and a few knights, and that was it. They stood there in their carefully arranged blocks, none cheering or calling out in joy, but watching in their finery, much as they might have done for an audience with the king. A priest stood up before the thrones, fat and bald and robed so that it looked a little like a tent standing there.

Finnal stood beside him, and even a few days ago, the sight of him there would have made Lenore's heart race with joy. Now, if it raced at all, there was fear there, and the need not to be there, and the part of her that thought it could look through that façade to what lay beneath.

Lenore glanced around, looking for a way out, but there was none.

Instead, she saw her sister Erin standing next to the man who looked like a monk. That was one thing that helped to calm her. She and Erin might not always have agreed on everything, but at least Lenore knew that Erin was always there for her. Just her presence helped Lenore feel safe. Even the monk's did, though Lenore knew now that he was not a monk, and had heard some of what he'd once been. He'd fought to save her, and that was enough.

Lenore came to stand before Finnal now, and Vars pulled back her veil, as if presenting her for his inspection. He went to stand beside the priest then, as if making it clear that it was by his will as much as any god's that this was happening. Lenore found herself staring at Finnal, trying to find the man that she'd fallen in love with, trying to persuade herself that things were as they had been.

"We are gathered here in somber celebration," the priest said. "These are days when we have all lost so much, but now there is a moment of joy, and joining. A moment of pure happiness."

Lenore wished she could feel any of those things.

The priest started to read through the vows, the promises to love one another, to be faithful, to be honorable and caring. Finnal agreed to all of it so readily that for a moment Lenore almost wanted to believe him. Even so, there was something about it now that sounded more like him agreeing to the terms of a contract than to love.

The priest turned to Lenore then, asking her all of the same things. The truth was that she was too numb to listen to any of it, too numb to do more than stare out at all the faces there, hoping that one of them would interrupt this, find a way to bring it to a—

"Princess?" the priest said. "Do you wish Finnal to be your husband?"

"I…I do," Lenore said. She couldn't think of anything else to say.

Bells rang in that moment, sounding out above the city. Now, briefly, people *did* cheer.

There was no dancing though, and no feasting. Instead, it seemed that those there were to take it in turns approaching, speaking to Vars and Finnal, only turning to her long enough to briefly compliment how beautiful she looked.

To her surprise, Lenore saw Devin walking forward then, a sheathed sword in his hands. Her heart leapt, thinking for a second that that he had come to save her from this. Instead, he knelt, holding up the sword toward Lenore.

"Your highness," he said. Something in his voice sounded stiff, almost stilted. "Your father and your brother had me forge this blade as a gift upon your wedding, for you to do with as you wish. I…I hope you will accept it in their honor."

Finnal stepped past Lenore, taking the sword from Devin's hands. He drew it, the darkness of the blade seeming almost to drink the light.

"A fine blade," he said. He slashed it through the air once again. "I will be delighted to accept it."

Lenore had to watch Devin backing away then, leaving the hall, the nobles, all of it.

Lenore wished for nothing more than to join him.

⚜ ⚜ ⚜

Lenore sat in the rooms that had been given to Finnal. He had assumed that they would go there, rather than to her rooms, so they had. She found herself sitting there, still in her wedding dress, while Finnal sat at a table with a ledger, hardly looking up at her as he made notes. This was hardly how she had expected her wedding night to go.

"Lord Harman's gift of two horses will go to the country estate," Finnal said. "They are not of the best stock, but they might be useful as an admixture in the bloodlines. We will need to send out riders to ensure that those on our new lands pay their taxes to us, rather than their old lords. Then there's the matter of–"

"Do you even care if I'm here?" Lenore asked. She stood. "I will be returning to my rooms."

"And have people think that we are spending our first night apart?" Finnal said, without looking up from the ledger. "I think not."

"Look at me, damn you!" Lenore snapped.

Finnal looked up, shutting the book carefully. "You are being petulant. I have told you how our marriage will be. You will accept that."

"I will not," Lenore said. Before, she'd only just come back from being in the hands of King Ravin's people. Before, she'd been too weak to say anything, but she could be strong. "I am going to my rooms. I am changing out of this stupid dress, and in the morning, I will be informing Vars that I wish this marriage annulled."

The sword that Devin had made sang from the scabbard at Finnal's side. He brought it to rest in the hollow of Lenore's throat, and she froze in place.

"You are my property now, Princess," he said menacingly, in a voice she barely recognized. "Take one step, and I shall cut your throat."

Chapter Thirty One

Greave hurried through Astare, Aurelle running to keep up in his wake. Around him, the city was a blur of leafy avenues and dark stone houses, but now each building there meant more. He could see now the way the buildings of the inner city fit together, parts of a whole, all a puzzle constructed on a massive scale.

"You don't have to run so fast!" Aurelle called behind him, but Greave didn't slow. He knew where the library was now, and he wasn't going to wait even one moment more to enter it.

"How do you even know we're going the right way?" she called over, catching up to him now.

"I memorized the map of the city," Greave said. "They haven't changed one stone of it since that map was built. Can you imagine the control of the city that must have taken?"

Aurelle didn't answer, obviously too busy running. They didn't have to run for too much longer, though, as they both reached the garden filled square that the map's clue had shown them. Greave scanned it, taking in the towering oaks there, the open ground, and the great stone gate that stood at the far end, next to a set of wrought iron railings that were more like a cage, designed to stop anyone from entering the space beyond. It looked like a monument or a grave, but Greave knew better now.

A bald, burly man sat on a bench nearby, ostensibly reading a book, yet Greave noted the way his eyes tracked them as he and Aurelle grew closer to the iron caged space beyond the gate. There, hidden by the shadows of the trees, underneath the iron bars, Greave thought he could see a slab that might be pushed aside.

"Interesting, isn't it?" the man on the bench called over, in a conversational tone. "Of course, once you realize that it's just the steps to the city's sewers ..."

That would probably be enough to turn away most people. Greave turned his gaze on the man instead. His clothes looked ordinary, but Greave could see the flash of silver on his shoes, too expensive for the man he was pretending to be.

"We seek entry to the Great Library of Astare," Greave said. "I know that the entrance is here."

"Ah," the man said. "That's different. You've passed one test, then. There's just the questioning to follow."

"The questioning?" Aurelle asked, beside Greave.

The bald man nodded. "The House of Scholars doesn't allow just anyone into its library. They must have enough learning to be worthy." The man stretched, setting his book aside. "I am Aldrin, tester of the House of Scholars. Who seeks entrance to our library?"

"I am Prince Greave," Greave answered. "My companion is Aurelle Hardacre."

"And what do you seek here, Prince Greave?"

"Knowledge," Greave said. "Of the scale sickness."

"Ah," Aldrin said. "Still, the questioning is traditional. Traditionally it's three, or until I'm satisfied. And don't try to bribe me. Folk who value money more than knowledge have no place here."

"I wasn't planning to," Greave said.

"And according to Vessimus, what are the three things that a man must seek?"

He asked the question as if it were nothing, yet the book was one Greave couldn't have imagined most people having read. Thankfully, Greave had read it, and many others.

"Honor, Knowledge, and the Benefit of Humanity," Greave answered. "Although his student Tarrin renders the last as Goodness."

Aldrin nodded. "And if I distill sweetrock using van Mer's process, what do I end up with?"

Greave thought for a moment, having to piece things together. He wasn't sure that he'd heard of sweetrock until he remembered that it was a name for natrium used in one of the Seven Poems of Kerric, and van Mer's process.

"Unless you're lucky, you end up with a hole where your alchemical bench used to be," Greave said. "Van Mer's process involves initial immersion in water, and natrium explodes in water."

"Hmm," Aldrin said with another nod. "Finally, in the third year, how many sons did King Jurin have?"

The third year? Greave's mind scrambled for an answer. "That's a trick question," he said at last. "You're hoping that someone will say that Jurin reigned in the sixtieth year of the two kingdoms being split."

"Am I?" Aldrin asked.

"But in his fortieth year, he went mad. He declared that the world had to begin again, and he ordered the calendar reset. His sons rebelled against him, and he killed one in the second year of the war. So by the third year, he had two left."

Aldrin nodded. "The questioning is complete. You may not enter."

"What?" It was what Greave was thinking, but it was Aurelle who said it, stepping past Greave. "He answered your questions. He got them right, I take it?"

Aldrin nodded. "But what you seek also matters, and so does being a member of the House. You may not enter."

"No," Greave said, all the air seeming to rush out of him at once. This ... this wasn't fair. Of course, a hundred philosophers sprang to mind who could tell him that the world wasn't fair, but this ... "I came here to save my sister," he said. Tears stung his eyes. In that moment, he felt utterly broken. "I—"

"None of that matters," Aldrin said. He held up a hand. "Step away now, or—"

"You'll let us in," Aurelle said, stepping closer to the man. To Greave's shock, a knife seemed almost to spring into her hand, a slender thing that definitely wasn't for eating, just for killing. She pressed it to the scholar's throat, starting to move him back toward the gate.

Greave couldn't contain his shock at that. "Aurelle? What are you doing?"

"Something I *shouldn't* be doing," she said. "Greave is a good man, trying to do a great thing. He's traveled for *days*, fought monsters, to be here. He's answered your *stupid* questions. Now let him—"

Bells sounded all around the city, interrupting Aurelle, making her step back from the scholar. He looked shocked, but it was hard to tell if that was because of her threat or because of the sounds of peeling chimes on every side.

People poured from buildings all around, some of them running toward the walls of the city, more of them heading toward the gates. They pushed at one another in panic, fighting as they tried to get clear.

"What is it?" Greave asked. "What's happening?"

"The bells," Aldrin said. "They signal attack, but that...that's *impossible*!"

The stone slab within the cage moved, shoved aside more lightly than should have been possible. There were stairs beneath, carved from stone. Figures ran up the stairs from the library below. Each wore the robes of the House of Scholars, and each looked as panicked as the others in the city. Greave could understand why: the Northern Kingdom was supposed to be safe, and somewhere this far north, this far from the threat of the Southern Kingdom, should have been the safest place of all.

Aldrin turned, ignoring Greave and Aurelle as he opened the gates to the library, letting the scholars out.

"We must flee the city now," he said to them. "We can return after the battle—if there is anything left to return to."

His men stared back, dumbfounded, in shock.

"RUN!" Aldrin called to his men, sprinting from the place as his men followed.

Greave watched them go, stunned. Before him, the gates now stood ajar.

"Greave," Aurelle said. She pulled at his arm. "If someone's attacking, we *have* to go."

Greave shook his head.

"You know how important this is."

"I know," she said. "But—"

"If you want to run, you can," Greave said. "Maybe you should. You'll be safer that way, but I can't. I *can't,* you understand?"

"I..." Aurelle nodded. "I understand. I...I'll stay. Wherever you are, I'll be."

Greave was instantly grateful for that.

He could hear the army coming, but the answers he sought lay below. If there was a cure to be found anywhere, it would be here; the notes he'd found in the castle library all but promised it.

He knew it was death to remain behind, yet he knew to flee would mean his sister's death.

And so with one bold step, Greave opened the gates, let himself and Aurelle inside, and slammed them behind him.

The answer lay before him. And he would find it, whatever the cost.

Chapter Thirty Two

Devin carefully packed away the forge on the castle's lower level, taking his time about it, not sure what else he should be doing. Above him, the sounds of the castle continued, but insulated from him by layer upon layer of stone, along, perhaps with some of Master Grey's enchantments.

Devin studied those, tracing them with his fingers, trying to understand them. When Master Grey had told him that he would need to learn something about magic, he had assumed it would mean learning runes like this, or chanting strange chants. Instead, he'd had him forge a sword.

Now it was forged, and Devin wasn't sure where he was supposed to go.

He set off up the steps from the forge, taking them slowly, seeing no point in hurrying now. He couldn't go home; his father had made that much abundantly clear. Would there be a place for him around the castle? Not that long before, the answer would have been obvious. When Rodry had been alive, he was there to be generous to his friends. Even the king might have shown some kindness to the smith who had obeyed his commands. Now, without them, Devin depended on Master Grey to say whether he could stay or not.

He came out into the sunlight, glancing up at the walls and hoping that he would catch a glimpse of Lenore there. There was one reason at least that he wanted to stay more than anything, yet maybe that was a reason he should go, too. Every thought he had seemed to be of Lenore, yet she was married to Finnal now. Devin had even given the sword to him at their wedding. Of course he would be the one to end up with both Lenore and the finest weapon Devin had ever seen; he looked like everything that a prince out of legend could be. Devin ... he was no more than a smith who no longer even had a place in the House of Weapons, given purpose only because Master Grey had wanted someone to work star metal.

Devin turned his eyes toward the sorcerer's tower, thinking of the things he had read there. Perhaps he would be better off plunging back into the city, away from everything the sorcerer had in mind for him. He could find work somewhere, perhaps in a village where a smith's skills could be put to use making horseshoes and fixing plows.

That would mean going away from all of this though, away from Lenore. Could Devin really do that?

He tried. He walked from the castle gates, heading down into the city, over the first of the bridges there, then the next. Each step felt like Devin was dragging a lead weight, though, or fighting against a chain pulling him in the other direction. He made it as far as the marketplace in the shadow of the House of Merchants before he stopped, knowing that he could not bring himself to go further.

Around him, the stalls were busy, people pushing and bumping as they strove to get the best bargains for themselves. Hawkers cried out the benefits of their wares compared to those of all the others there. Burly porters lifted crates. In one corner, a pen held sheep, men crowded round them for an auction.

Devin stood there in the middle of it, and yet he didn't feel like a part of any of it. Yes, he could walk away, could go to some village somewhere, or even get on a boat to far off Sarras, but what good would it really do him? He had tasted what it was like to be different now, had felt the power inside him pouring into metal and shaping it. He'd even somehow thrown back the wolves that had come at them in Clearwater Deep. Swordmaster Wendros had told him that he would never be a swordsman or a knight, but maybe he had found his own niche in the world.

Devin stood in the crowd, but he knew then that he would never feel a part of it again.

Then there was Lenore, whose image still haunted Devin's mind even as he tried to walk away. Leaving Royalsport wouldn't just mean leaving behind the promise of a life that was something different, something more. It would mean leaving her there in the castle, alone. It would mean a lifetime thinking of her, and yet never seeing her.

His mind made up, Devin turned back toward the castle.

There was a space in the crowds of the marketplace now, perfectly circular, admitting no people. The strangeness of it caught Devin's eye, because people packed in on every other side, barely an inch of ground not taken up by someone in the bustle of the market. Even Devin had to push and twist his way between people, yet not one person set foot in that open circle. The strangest thing was that they didn't even seem to notice that it was there. They walked around it without even looking into it, glanced to neighbors instead, pushed others aside rather than risk walking in the space.

Devin looked into it though, and at its heart, he saw a single figure, in robes of white and gold, sitting upon what appeared to be an abandoned crate of apples. He was eating one of them, and that seemed almost as incongruous for Master Grey as the strange empty circle he was somehow maintaining for himself.

Devin pushed forward, fighting his way into that circle. As he met its edge, there was a brief moment of resistance, his thoughts trying to tell him that there was no circle, that he was imagining it all, that there were some lovely sides of mutton just over there that he should—

He took another step, and the sensation was gone. He stood over Master Grey, who sat there calmly, tossing away the half-eaten apple and looking up at him.

"What are you doing *here*?" Devin demanded. "You haven't been in your tower. You weren't there for the forging of the sword, or for the return from the battle, or any of it."

Around them, the people continued to flow, giving no sign that they'd heard Devin raise his voice.

"I was where I needed to be," Master Grey said. "And I am now."

There it was, an answer and not an answer, like always. It was enough to make Devin turn for the edge of the circle again.

"You already decided not to do that," Master Grey pointed out.

"How can you know what I've decided?" Devin demanded, turning back to the sorcerer.

Master Grey shrugged. "This is the spot where you decide. Had you kept walking, you would not have seen me here, and I would have been forced to find... another. As it is, you realized how important destiny is, and so you turned back."

Devin thought of Lenore again, of her sitting there in the castle, of her sadness, of her beauty. "It wasn't about destiny."

"You may believe that," Master Grey said. "I do not have that luxury."

"What do you want?" Devin asked. "You talk in riddles, but you never say what you want out of all this."

"I want what I have always wanted: what is best for this kingdom, and for humanity," Master Grey said, his expression suddenly piercing. "I want you to be all that has been promised. I want what is to come to be something the world we know can survive."

"And what's coming?" Devin demanded.

Master Grey shook his head and sighed. "Too much."

"That's not an answer."

"We don't *get* answers!" Master Grey snapped back, and it was so rare to hear him raise his voice that way that Devin took a step back in shock. "Even I only get fragments of it, to piece together as best I can. We perform our parts in this, and hope that it is enough."

Devin bit back his anger. There was no point trying to argue with the magus; it would only mean more riddles, never a real answer.

"And what's my part in this?" he asked.

"For now," Master Grey said, "it is to return to the castle. There will be rooms there for you for as long as I wish it."

"And then?" Devin asked. "I'm not going back unless you tell me more."

"You will," Master Grey said. "For her."

He didn't need to say who he meant; they both knew. Devin didn't ask how he knew what he felt about Lenore, either. It seemed that Master Grey knew plenty of things he shouldn't.

The sorcerer stood, grasping Devin by the shoulders. "Forging the first sword has taught you the skills you need, but it is just a beginning. The Unfinished Sword... the sword of all swords... it must be found. And it must be finished. And only you are made for this task."

He stepped away from Devin then, striding into the crowd. The bubble of space around him seemed to burst as soon as he stepped from it, people crowding in around Devin too tightly for him to follow the sorcerer. His mind was still reeling.

"What unfinished sword?" he called out over the crowd, but there was no answer.

The sorcerer was already gone.

Chapter Thirty Three

"There will be a celebration at the turning of the moon," Lina said, and Nerra smiled. Her friend seemed always to look for bright things in the life of the island.

"What is there to celebrate here?" Nerra asked, grinding corn with a quern, the heavy stone scraping down upon it as she and Lina walked it around and around. Today, they were working on milling flour to bake with, helping to produce the bread and cakes that their small community needed.

"That we are still here," Lina said. "That there are still things in life that are joyful."

It was hard to be sad when Lina was around. It seemed that even the most bestial of those with the dragon sickness brightened up as she passed. Nerra wished that she had the same gift, but every second seemed to fill itself with thoughts of the home she had lost, the family that she would never see. Would Lenore be married now? Would Erin have come back from wherever she had run to?

"Here, let me help you," Nerra said as Lina started to lift a completed sack from her side. She went over, helping her friend with the weight of it, the two of them taking it toward a pile of similar sacks out in the open air of the village.

They'd only gone a few steps before Lina stopped.

"I don't feel..."

Something twitched in her face, the lines of the dragon sickness seeming to shift and move across her skin. Nerra stared in horror as her friend's features seemed to move like water affected by a breeze. Lina cried out, fell to her kneels, collapsed.

Nerra felt as though her heart was being torn out as she watched Lina writhing on the floor, her body seeming to twist out of shape even as she watched. One arm seemed to crack and twist, becoming something *else*, while her eyes stared up in horror, eerily the same as they had been before.

The attack had come out of nowhere. One moment, the two had been working together in the village, the next, Lina was screaming. She was doubled over in agony now on the floor, hands clutching her belly. A few seconds later, and Nerra was staring down at her newly acquired friend, watching her body tear itself to pieces.

Finally, she fought past her shock enough to cry out, to seek help.

"Kleos!" she called out. "Somebody fetch Kleos!"

She could already see him from the corner of her eye, running toward this, trying to get there in time to help. All the while, though, Lina was screaming, until even her screams broke into something else, something guttural and strange and twisted.

Kleos stood over her, staring down, his face filled with pity. "It…this happens sometimes. The sickness can be held at bay for years, then come upon someone in a rush to try to transform them."

His words were tinged with sadness, but it didn't seem like enough to Nerra. He wasn't doing anything, wasn't trying to change anything, wasn't trying to *help* her.

"Why are you just standing there?" Nerra demanded.

"This is the dragon sickness at work," Kleos said. "There is nothing that *can* be done."

On the ground before Nerra, Lina continued to shift and change, utterly inhuman now.

"She will not survive," Kleos said. "She has no strength to withstand the change."

He said that like he was observing an animal in the wild, not looking down over the body of a young woman who had supposedly been there on the island with him for years. It wasn't that there was no pity there, but there seemed to be something resigned about it, something that merely accepted the inevitability of what was to come.

"No," Nerra said. "You have to help her. You have to *do* something."

It was too late, though. Nerra could see the way that Lina's flesh was pulling itself apart, see the great tears in it now. For a moment, a rent appeared in her flesh that seemed to show Nerra the inner workings of her body, even the beating of her heart, frantic and fluttering, struggling to keep up.

Then that heart stopped.

"No," Nerra said, looking away. "No."

"It is a sad moment for us all," Kleos said. "But you must remember that–"

"Don't you *dare* say anything!" Nerra snapped back at him, pointing one accusing finger. "Don't you dare! She was my friend, was kind and gentle, and you just stood there watching her die like even *comfort* was beyond you."

"I have seen more death than you ever will," Kleos said. There were tears in his eyes, but they were nothing compared to the ones in Nerra's. "Do you think if I weep for all of them, it makes it any better? I'll be here watching over this island long after the dragon sickness claims you!"

Yes, he would. He would be here, and Nerra… She looked back at the body of her friend, but she couldn't bear to look for long. Not when the dragon sickness had taken her friend from her so brutally, and so utterly.

Nerra had thought she might have years here, thought she might be able to come to terms with it, as Lina seemed to have. Now, she had seen firsthand just how swiftly, and how brutally, the sickness could strike.

She knew what she had to do. Even the death Kleos had warned about the waters bringing was better than *this.*

⚜ ⚜ ⚜

Nerra walked across the island, the heat bearing down on her. It seemed to grow as she crossed the slopes of the volcano, walking without stopping, knowing that if she stopped, she might lose her nerve to do this.

She had to do this, because the alternative was just sitting and waiting for death. All her life, Nerra had tried to learn about the world, tried to help and heal others. She couldn't accept a world where death could just snatch at her at any moment.

The way was treacherous beneath her feet. Nerra found her footing giving way every few steps, the rocky slopes of the mountainside uneven, the slope itself steep enough that it was hard to think of the way she was walking as a path.

Yet there *was* a path, leveled into the slope, only broken here and there by fallen rocks, some larger than Nerra herself. The sight of them made Nerra look up the slope, and it was that which saved her. She saw a tumble of rocks heading down toward her, each large enough to easily kill her if it struck her. She ducked out of the way just in time, watching the boulders roll on past.

She kept going, yet one thing seemed determined to stop her: a pain that started as a dull ache inside her, but seemed to grow with every step. Strangely, it receded when Nerra backed away a pace or two, but grew again when she kept going, almost as if there was something there pushing her back, trying to keep her from her destination.

Nerra didn't stop though, just gritted her teeth and kept going.

The pain built, and built, so that it felt as though every part of her was pulling in a different direction. The world seemed to swim in front of her eyes, and her body seemed to long for her to stop. Nerra stared at her arms, fully expecting them to be twisted and misshapen, the way Lina's had been. No, though, this wasn't the scale sickness killing her; this was a purer kind of pain that had nothing to do with it, and everything to do with whatever force was trying to keep her back.

Nerra fought her way on, step by step, stride by stride. On this side of the volcano, there were live patches of lava, forming pools crossed by basalt spans that looked as though they might fall away at any moment. She kept going past them, crying out with agony now, but not stopping.

She saw it then, round a bend in the track, a structure of black pillars that seemed to have an impossibly green space within, while all around it was empty rock. At the heart of that was a circle of more black stone, from which water bubbled up in a fountain, falling into a pool around it.

With that target in mind, Nerra forced her way forward, eyes on the pool. One step, then another, getting closer to the pillars with each one. Her hand found the black stone there…

Instantly, the pain vanished, leaving Nerra to stumble forward onto the grass around the fountain. She knelt there for a moment, looking around, and that was when she saw the bones. They lay scattered in piles around the fountain, bleached white by the sun but otherwise untouched. They had to be those who had come to the fountain before, the ones who had been so sure they would survive, the ones who had needed its cure so badly.

Nerra could feel the fear of that welling within her. She knew that the waters here might well kill her, could see the evidence all around her. Was she really arrogant enough to believe that she might survive the deadliness of the waters? Wasn't it better just to turn back, to live out her life ...

"No!" Nerra shouted, forcing herself on.

She didn't dare to stop, instead crawling forward until she pulled herself up to the lip of the fountain, looking down into the waters that sprang up there. They were clear and deep, with no sign of anything within them other than the reflection of Nerra's features. Nerra gasped as she saw them, and the way the scale mark had crept its way onto her features in the time that she'd been there. She touched a hand to it, imagining all the ways it might change her, all the horrors that it might inflict upon her flesh.

That gave Nerra the courage to do what she hadn't been sure she would do, even now. She had no wish to end up like Lina, destroyed by her own body, or like one of the bestial things that Kleos put down with his blade. She wanted to be free of this sickness, free to go home. She wanted to see her sisters again.

Nerra dipped her hands into the water. It was warmer than she had thought it would be, although that might just be the effects of the volcano close by, with nothing magical about it at all. What if that was really all it was? A pool poisoned by the volcano's minerals, with stories linked to it for so long that it still gave hope to the hopeless.

Even then, it would be better than the alternative.

Cupping her hands together, Nerra drank.

Now Available for Pre-Order!

BORN OF DRAGONS
(Age of the Sorcerers—Book Three)

"Has all the ingredients for an instant success: plots, counterplots, mystery, valiant knights, and blossoming relationships replete with broken hearts, deception and betrayal. It will keep you entertained for hours, and will satisfy all ages. Recommended for the permanent library of all fantasy readers."

—Books and Movie Reviews, Roberto Mattos (re *The Sorcerer's Ring*)

"The beginnings of something remarkable are there."

—San Francisco Book Review (re *A Quest of Heroes*)

From #1 bestseller Morgan Rice, author of *A Quest of Heroes* (over 1,300 five star reviews) comes the debut of a startlingly new fantasy series.

BORN OF DRAGONS (Age of the Sorcerers—Book Three) tells the story of the epic coming of age of one very special 16 year old boy, a blacksmith's son from a poor family who is offered no chance of proving his fighting skills and breaking into the ranks of the nobles. Yet he holds a power he cannot deny, and a fate he must follow.

It tells the story of a 17 year old princess on the eve of her wedding, destined for greatness—and of her younger sister, rejected by her family and dying of plague.

It tells the tale of their three brothers, three princes who could not be more different from each other—all of them vying for power.

It tells the story of a kingdom on the verge of change, of invasion, the story of the dying dragon race, falling daily from the sky.

It tells the tale of two rival kingdoms, of the rapids dividing them, of a landscape dotted with dormant volcanoes, and of a capital accessible only with the tides. It is a story of love, passion, of hate and sibling rivalry; of rogues and hidden treasure; of monks and secret warriors; of honor and glory, and of betrayal and deception.

It is the story of Dragonfell, a story of honor and valor, of sorcerers, magic, fate and destiny. It is a tale you will not put down until the early hours, one that will transport you to another world and have you fall in in love with characters you will never forget. It appeals to all ages and genders.

Book four will soon be available for pre-order.

"A spirited fantasy....Only the beginning of what promises to be an epic young adult series."

—Midwest Book Review (re *A Quest of Heroes*)

"Action-packed.... Rice's writing is solid and the premise intriguing."

—Publishers Weekly (re *A Quest of Heroes*)

BORN OF DRAGONS
(Age of the Sorcerers—Book Three)

Did you know that I've written multiple series? If you haven't read all my series, click the image below to download a series starter!

Printed in Great Britain
by Amazon

30483772R00108